The Mask of Cthulhu

August Derleth

Carroll & Graf Publishers, Inc.
New York

Originally published by Arkham House Publishers in 1958. This edition published by arrangement with the author's estate.

First Carroll & Graf edition 1996.

Carroll & Graf Publishers, Inc.
260 Fifth Avenue
New York, NY 10001

ISBN 0-7867-0337-7

Manufactured in the United States of America.

Contents

Introduction

THE NARRATIVES in this book are, manifestly, on Lovecraftian themes. Indeed, one of them—*The Return of Hastur*—was begun before the death of H. P. Lovecraft, who saw its opening pages and the outline of my proposed development, and in consequence made several suggestions which were enthusiastically incorporated into the story. The remaining stories also stem directly from the Cthulhu Mythos created by Lovecraft, who was in the habit of urging his writer friends to add to and expand the Mythos.

These tales were written over a period of roughly two decades, beginning with *The Return of Hastur* in 1936, and ending with *The Seal of R'lyeh*, which was conceived and written in Los Angeles in the summer of 1953. While all the stories owe their existence to the myth-pattern created by Lovecraft, one, *The House in the Valley*, had its inception in a sketch of the setting taken from an actual scene by the well-known artist-cartoonist, Richard Taylor, whose jacket wraps around this book.

The stories in these pages represent, as it were, a postscript in tribute to the creative imagination of the late H. P. Lovecraft.

—AUGUST DERLETH

The Return of Hastur

ACTUALLY, IT BEGAN a long time ago: how long, I have not dared to guess: but so far as is concerned my own connection with the case that has ruined my practice and earned me the dubiety of the medical profession in regard to my sanity, it began with Amos Tuttle's death. That was on a night in late winter, with a south wind blowing on the edge of spring. I had been in ancient, legend-haunted Arkham that day; he had learned of my presence there from Doctor Ephraim Sprague, who attended him, and had the doctor call the Lewiston House and bring me to that gloomy estate on the Aylesbury Road near the Innsmouth Turnpike. It was not a place to which I liked to go, but the old man had paid me well to tolerate his sullenness and eccentricity, and Sprague had made it clear that he was dying: a matter or hours.

And he was. He had hardly the strength to motion Sprague from the room and talk to me, though his voice came clearly enough and with little effort.

"You know my will," he said. "Stand by it to the letter."

That will had been a bone of contention between us because of its provision that before his heir and sole surviving nephew, Paul Tuttle, could claim his estate, the house would have to be destroyed—not taken down, but destroyed, together with certain books designated by shelf number in his final instructions. His death-bed was no place to debate this wanton destruction anew; I nodded, and he accepted that. Would to heaven I had obeyed without question!

"Now then," he went on, "there's a book downstairs you must take back to the library of Miskatonic University."

He gave me the title. At that time it meant little to me; but it has since come to mean more than I can say—a symbol of age-old horror, of maddening things beyond the thin veil of prosaic daily life—the Latin translation of the abhorred *Necronomicon* by the mad Arab, Abdul Alhazred.

I found the book easily enough. For the last two decades of his life Amos Tuttle had lived in increasing seclusion among books collected from all parts of the world: old, worm-eaten texts, with titles that might have frightened away a less hardened man—the sinister *De Vermis Mysteriis* of Ludvig Prinn, Comte d'Erlette's terrible *Cultes de Ghoules,* von Junzt's damnable *Unaussprechlichen Kulten.* I did not then know how rare these were, nor did I understand the priceless rarity of certain fragmentary pieces: the frightful *Book of Eibon,* the horror-fraught *Pnakotic Manuscripts,* and the dread *R'lyeh Text;* for these, I found upon an examination of his accounts after Amos Tuttle's death, he had paid a fabulous sum. But nowhere did I find so high a figure as that he had paid for the *R'lyeh Text,* which had come to him from somewhere in the dark interior of Asia; according to his files, he had paid for it no less than one hundred thousand dollars; but in addition to this, there was present in his account in regard to this yellowed manuscript a notation which puzzled me at the time, but which I was to have ominous cause to remember—after the sum above mentioned, Amos Tuttle had written in his spidery hand: *in addition to the promise.*

These facts did not come out until Paul Tuttle was in possession, but before that, several strange occurrences took place, things that should have aroused my suspicion in regard to the countryside legends of some powerful supernatural influence clinging to the old house. The first of these was of small consequence in view of the others; it was simply that upon returning the *Necronomicon* to the library of Miskatonic University at Arkham, I found myself conveyed by a tight-lipped librarian straightway to the office of the director, Doctor Llanfer, who asked me bluntly to account for the book's being in my hands. I had no hesitation in doing so, and thereby discovered that the rare volume was never permitted out of the library, that, in fact, Amos Tuttle had abstracted it on one of his rare visits, having failed in his attempts to persuade Doctor Llanfer to permit his borrowing it. And Amos had been clever enough to prepare in advance a marvelously good imitation of the book, with a binding almost flawless in its resemblance, and the actual reproduction of title and opening pages of the text reproduced from his memory; upon the occasion of his handling the mad Arab's book, he had substituted his dummy for the original and gone off with one of the two copies of this shunned work available on the North American continent, one of the five copies known to be in existence in the world.

The second of these things was a little more startling, though it bears the trappings of conventional haunted house stories. Both Paul Tuttle and I heard at odd times in the house at night, while his uncle's corpse lay there particularly, the sound of

padding footsteps, but there was this strangeness about them:
they were not like footsteps falling within the house at all, but
like the steps of some creature in size almost beyond the conception of man walking at a great distance *underground,* so
that the sound actually *vibrated* into the house from the depths
of earth below. And when I have reference to steps, it is only
for lack of a better word to describe the sounds, for they were
not flat steps at all, but a kind of spongy, jelly-like, sloshing
sound made with the force of so much weight behind them that
the consequent shuddering of earth in that place was communi-
cated to us in the way we heard it. There was nothing more
than this, and presently it was gone, ceasing, coincidentally
enough, in the hours of that dawn when Amos Tuttle's corpse
was borne away forty-eight hours sooner than we had planned.
The sounds we dismissed as settlings of the earth along the
distant coast, not alone because we did not attach too great an
importance to them, but because of the final thing that took
place before Paul Tuttle officially took possession of the old
house on the Aylesbury Road.

This last thing was the most shocking of all, and of the
three who knew it, only I now remain alive, Doctor Sprague
being dead this day month, though he took only one look and
said, "Bury him at once!" And so we did, for the change in
Amos Tuttle's body was ghastly beyond conception, and especially horrible in its suggestion, and it was so because the body
was *not* falling into any visible decay, but changing subtly in
another way, becoming suffused with a weird iridescence, which
darkened presently until it was almost ebon, and the appearance
on the flesh of his puffy hands and face of minute, scale-like
growth. There was likewise some change about the shape of

his head; it seemed to lengthen, to take on a curious kind of
fish-like look, accompanied by a faint exudation of thick fish
smell from the coffin; and that these changes were not purely
imaginative was shockingly substantiated when the body was
subsequently found in the place where its malignant after-
dweller had conveyed it, and there, at last falling into putre-
faction though it was, others saw with me the terrible, suggestive changes that had taken place, though they had mercifully no knowledge of what had gone before. But at the time
when Amos Tuttle lay in the old house, there was no hint of
what was to come; we were quick to close the coffin and quicker
still to take it to the ivy-covered Tuttle vault in Arkham cemetery.

Paul Tuttle was at that time in his late forties, but, like so
many men of his generation, he had the face and figure of a
youth in his twenties. Indeed, the only hint of his age lay in the
faint traces of gray in the hair of his moustache and temples.
He was a tall, dark-haired man, slightly overweight, with frank
blue eyes which years of scholarly research had not reduced to
the necessity of glasses. Nor was he ignorant of law, for he
quickly made known that if I, as his uncle's executor, were
not disposed to overlook the clause in his will that called for
the destruction of the house on the Aylesbury Road, he would
contest the will on the justifiable ground of Amos Tuttle's
insanity. I pointed out to him that he stood alone against
Doctor Sprague and me, but I was at the same time not blind
to the fact that the unreasonableness of the request might very
well defeat us; besides, I myself considered the clause in this
regard amazingly wanton in the destruction it demanded, and
was not prepared to fight a contest because of so minor a

matter. Yet, could I have foreseen what was to come, could I have dreamed of the horror to follow, I would have carried out Amos Tuttle's last request regardless of any decision of the court. However, such foresight was not mine.

We went to see Judge Wilton, Tuttle and I, and put the matter before him. He agreed with us that the destruction of the house seemed needless, and more than once hinted at concurrence with Paul Tuttle's belief in his late uncle's madness.

"The old man's been touched for as long as I knew him," he said dryly. "And as for you, Haddon, can you get up on a stand and swear that he was absolutely sane?"

Remembering with a certain uneasiness the theft of the *Necronomicon* from Miskatonic University, I had to confess that I could not.

So Paul Tuttle took possession of the estate on the Aylesbury road, and I went back to my legal practice in Boston, not dissatisfied with the way things had gone, and yet not without a lurking uneasiness difficult to define, an insidious feeling of impending tragedy, no little fed by my memory of what we had seen in Amos Tuttle's coffin before we sealed and locked it away in the centuries-old vault in Arkham cemetery.

2

It was not for some time that I saw the gambrel roofs and Georgian balustrades of witch-cursed Arkham again, and then was there on business for a client who wished me to see to it that his property in ancient Innsmouth was protected from the Government agents and police who had taken possession of the shunned and haunted town, though it was now some months since the mysterious dynamiting of blocks of the waterfront buildings and part of the terror-hung Devil Reef in the sea beyond—a mystery which has been carefully guarded and hidden since then, though I have learned of a paper purporting to give the true facts of the Innsmouth horror, a privately published manuscript written by a Providence author. It was impossible at that time to proceed to Innsmouth because Secret Service men had closed all roads; however, I made representations to the proper persons and received an assurance that my client's property would be fully protected, since it lay well back from the waterfront; so I proceeded about other small matters in Arkham.

I went to luncheon that day in a small restaurant near Miskatonic University, and while there, heard myself accosted in a familiar voice. I looked up and saw Doctor Llanfer, the university library's director. He seemed somewhat upset, and betrayed his concern clearly in his features. I invited him to join me, but he declined; he did, however, sit down, somewhat on the chair's edge.

"Have you been out to see Paul Tuttle?" he asked abruptly.

"I thought of going this afternoon," I replied. "Is anything wrong?"

He flushed a little guiltily. "That I can't say," he answered precisely. "But there have been some nasty rumors loose in Arkham. And the *Necronomicon* is gone again."

"Good Heaven! you're surely not accusing Paul Tuttle of having taken it?" I exclaimed, half in surprise, half amused. "I could not imagine of what use it might be to him."

"Still—he has it," Doctor Llanfer persisted. "But I don't think he stole it, and should not like to be understood as saying so. It is my opinion that one of our clerks gave it to him and is now reluctant to confess the enormity of his error. Be that as it may, the book has not come back, and I fear we shall have to go after it."

"I could ask him about it," I said.

"If you would, thank you," responded Doctor Llanfer, a little eagerly. "I take it you've heard nothing of the rumors that are rife here?"

I shook my head.

"Very likely they are only the outgrowth of some imaginative mind," he continued, but the air of him suggested that he was not willing or able to accept so prosaic an explanation. "It appears that passengers along the Aylesbury Road have heard strange sounds late at night, all apparently emanating from the Tuttle house."

"What sounds?" I asked, not without immediate apprehension.

"Apparently those of footsteps; and yet, I understand no one will definitely say so, save for one young man who characterized them as *soggy* and said that they sounded as if *something big were walking in mud and water near by.*"

The strange sounds Paul Tuttle and I had heard on the night following Amos Tuttle's death had passed from my mind, but at this mention of footsteps by Doctor Llanfer, the memory of what I had heard returned in full. I fear I gave myself slightly away, for Doctor Llanfer observed my sudden interest; fortunately, he chose to interpret it as evidence that I had indeed heard something of these rumors, my statement to the contrary notwithstanding. I did not choose to correct him in this regard, and at the same time I experienced a sudden desire to hear no more; so I did not press him for further details, and presently he rose to return to his duties, and left me with my promise to ask Paul Tuttle for the missing book still sounding in my ears.

His story, however slight it was, nevertheless sounded within me a note of alarm; I could not help recalling the numerous small things that held to memory—the steps we had heard, the odd clause in Amos Tuttle's will, the awful metamorphosis in Amos Tuttle's corpse. There was already then a faint suspicion in my mind that some sinister chain of events was becoming manifest here; my natural curiosity rose, though not without a certain feeling of distaste, a conscious desire to withdraw, and the recurrence of that strange, insidious conviction of impending tragedy. But I determined to see Paul Tuttle as early as possible.

My work in Arkham consumed the afternoon, and it was not until dusk that I found myself standing before the massive oaken door of the old Tuttle house on Aylesbury Road. My rather peremptory knock was answered by Paul himself, who stood, lamp held high in hand, peering out into the growing night.

"Haddon!" he exclaimed, throwing the door wider. "Come in!"

That he was genuinely glad to see me I could not doubt, for the note of enthusiasm in his voice precluded any other supposition. The heartiness of his welcome also served to confirm me in my intention not to speak of the rumors I had heard, and to proceed about an inquiry after the *Necronomicon* at my own good time. I remembered that just prior to his uncle's death, Tuttle had been working on a philological treatise relating to the growth of the Sac Indian language, and determined to inquire about this paper as if nothing else were of moment.

"You've had supper, I suppose," said Tuttle, leading me down the hall and into the library.

I said that I had eaten in Arkham.

He put the lamp down upon a book-laden table, pushing some papers to one side as he did so. Inviting me to sit down, he resumed the seat he had evidently left to answer my knock. I saw now that he was somewhat disheveled, and that he had permitted his beard to grow. He had also taken on more weight, doubtless as a consequence of strictly enforced scholarship, with all its attendant confinement to the house and lack of physical exercise.

"How fares the Sac treatise?" I asked.

"I've put that aside," he said shortly. "I may take it up later. For the present, I've struck something far more important —just how important I cannot yet say."

I saw now that the books on the tables were not the usual scholarly tomes I had seen on his Ipswich desk, but with some faint apprehension observed that they were the books condemned by the explicit instructions of Tuttle's uncle, as a glance at the vacant spaces on the proscribed shelves clearly corroborated.

Tuttle turned to me almost eagerly and lowered his voice as if in fear of being overheard. "As a matter of fact, Haddon, it's colossal—a gigantic feat of the imagination; only for this: I'm no longer certain that it *is* imaginative, indeed, I'm not. I wondered about that clause in my uncle's will; I couldn't understand why he should want this house destroyed, and rightly surmised that the reason must lie somewhere in the pages of those books he so carefully condemned." He waved a hand at the incunabula before him. "So I examined them, and I can tell you I have discovered things of such incredible strangeness, such bizarre horror, that I hesitate sometimes to dig deeper into the mystery. Frankly, Haddon, it is the most *outré* matter I've ever come upon, and I must say it involved considerable research, quite apart from these books Uncle Amos collected."

"Indeed," I said dryly. "And I dare say you've had to do considerable travelling?"

He shook his head. "None at all, apart from one trip to Miskatonic University Library. The fact is, I found I could be served just as well by mail. You'll remember those papers of uncle's? Well, I discovered among them that Uncle Amos paid a hundred thousand for a certain bound manuscript— bound in human skin, incidentally—together with a cryptic line: *in addition to the promise.* I began to ask myself what promise Uncle Amos could have made, and to whom; whether to the man or woman who had sold him this *R'lyeh Text* or to some other. I proceeded forthwith to search out the name of the man who had sold him the book, and presently found it with his address: some Chinese priest from inner Tibet: and wrote to him. His reply reached me a week ago."

He bent away and rummaged briefly among the papers on his desk, until he found what he sought and handed it to me.

"I wrote in my uncle's name not trusting entirely in the transaction, and wrote, moreover, as if I had forgotten or had a hope to avoid the promise," he continued. "His reply is fully as cryptic as my uncle's notation."

Indeed, it was so, for the crumpled paper that was handed to me bore, in a strange, stilted script, but one line, without signature or date: *To afford a haven for Him Who is not to be Named.*

I dare say I looked up at Tuttle with my wonderment clearly mirrored in my eyes, for he smiled before he replied.

"Means nothing to you, eh? No more did it to me, when first I saw it. But not for long. In order to understand what follows, you should know at least a brief outline of the mythology—if indeed it *is* only mythology—in which this mystery is rooted. My Uncle Amos apparently knew and believed all about it, for the various notes scattered in the margins of his proscribed books bespeak a knowledge far beyond mine. Apparently the mythology springs from a common source with our own legendary Genesis, but only by a very thin resemblance; sometimes I am tempted to say that this mythology is far older than any other—certainly in its implications it goes far beyond, being cosmic and ageless, for its beings are of two natures, and two only: the Old or Ancient Ones, the Elder Gods, of *cosmic good*, and those of *cosmic evil*, bearing many names, and themselves of different groups, as if associated with the elements and yet transcending them: for there are the Water Beings, hidden in the depths; those of Air that are the primal lurkers beyond time; those of Earth, horrible animate survivals of distant eons. Incredible time ago, the Old Ones banished from the cosmic places all the Evil Ones, imprisoning them in many places; but in time these Evil Ones spawned hellish minions who set about preparing for their return to greatness. The Old Ones are nameless, but their power is and will apparently always be great enough to check that of the others.

"Now, among the Evil Ones there is apparently often conflict, as among lesser beings. The Water Beings oppose those of Air; the Fire Beings oppose Earth Beings, but nevertheless, they together hate and fear the Elder Gods and hope always to defeat them in some future time. Among my Uncle Amos's papers there are many fearsome names written in his crabbed script: *Great Cthulhu, the Lake of Hali, Tsathoggua, Yog-Sothoth, Nyarlathotep, Azathoth, Hastur the Unspeakable, Yuggoth, Aldones, Thale, Aldebaran, the Hyades, Carcosa,* and others: and it is possible to divide some of these names into vaguely suggestive classes from those notes which are explicable to me—though many present insoluble mysteries I cannot hope as yet to penetrate; and many, too, are written in a language I do not know, together with cryptic and oddly frightening symbols and signs. But through what I have learned, it is possible to know that Great Cthulhu is one of the Water Beings, even as Hastur is of the Beings that stalk the star-spaces; and it is possible to gather from vague hints in these forbidden books where some of these beings are. So I can believe that in this mythology, Great Cthulhu was banished to a place beneath the seas of Earth, while Hastur was hurled into outer space, into that *place where the black stars hang,* which is indicated as Aldebaran of the Hyades, which is the place mentioned by Chambers, even as he repeats the *Carcosa* of Bierce.

"Coming upon this communication from the priest in Tibet in the light of these things, surely one fact must come clearly forth: Haddon, surely, beyond the shadow of a doubt, He Who is not to be Named can be none other than Hastur the Unspeakable!"

The sudden cessation of his voice startled me; there was something hypnotic about his eager whisper, and something

too that filled me with a conviction far beyond the power of
Paul Tuttle's words. Somewhere, deep within the recesses of
my mind, a chord had been struck, a mnemonic connection I
could not dismiss or trace and which left me with a feeling
as of limitless age, a cosmic bridge into another place and time.

"That seems logical," I said at last, cautiously.

"Logical! Haddon, it *is;* it must be!" he exclaimed.

"Granting it," I said, "what then?"

"Why, granting it," he went on quickly, "we have conceded
that my Uncle Amos promised to make ready a haven in
preparation for the return of Hastur from whatever region
of outer space now imprisons him. Where that haven is, or
what manner of place it may be, has not thus far been my
concern, though I can guess, perhaps. This is not the time for
guessing, and yet it would seem, from certain other evidence
at hand, that there may be some permissible deductions made.
The first and most important of these is of a double nature—
ergo, something unforeseen prevented the return of Hastur
within my uncle's lifetime, and yet some other being has made
itself manifest." Here he looked at me with unusual frankness
and not a little nervousness. "As for the evidence of this manifestation, I would rather not at this time go into it. Suffice it
to say that I believe I have such evidence at hand. I return to
my original premise, then.

"Among the few marginal notations made by my uncle,
there are two or three especially remarkable ones in the
R'lyeh Text; indeed, in the light of what is known or can
justifiably be guessed, they are sinister and ominous notes."

So speaking, he opened the ancient manuscript and turned to
a place quite close to the beginning of the narrative.

"Now attend me, Haddon," he said, and I rose and bent over him to look at the spidery, almost illegible script that I knew for Amos Tuttle's. "Observe the underscored line of text: *Ph'nglui mglw'nafh Cthulhu R'lyeh wgah' nagl fhtagn,* and what follows it in my uncle's unmistakable hand: *His minions preparing the way, and he no longer dreaming?* (*WT: 2/28*) and at a more recent date, to judge by the shakiness of his hand, the single abbreviation: *Inns!* Obviously, this means nothing without a translation of the text. Failing this at the moment I first saw this note, I turned my attention to the parenthetical notation, and within a short while solved its meaning as a reference to a popular magazine, *Weird Tales,* for February, 1928. I have it here."

He opened the magazine against the meaningless text, partially concealing the lines which had begun to take on an uncanny atmosphere of eldritch age beneath my eyes, and there beneath Paul Tuttle's hand lay the first page of a story so obviously belonging to this unbelievable mythology that I could not repress a start of astonishment. The title, only partly covered by his hand, was *The Call of Cthulhu,* by H. P. Lovecraft. But Tuttle did not linger over the first page; he turned well into the heart of the story before he paused and presented to my gaze the identical unreadable line that lay beside the crabbed script of Amos Tuttle in the incredibly rare *R'lyeh Text* upon which the magazine reposed. And there, only a paragraph below, appeared what purported to be a translation of the utterly unknown language of the *Text: In his house at R'lyeh dead Cthulhu waits dreaming.*

"There you have it," resumed Tuttle with some satisfaction. "Cthulhu, too, waited for the time of his resurgence—how many eons, no one may know; but my uncle has questioned whether Cthulhu still lies dreaming, and following this, has written and doubly underscored an abbreviation which can only stand for *Innsmouth!* This, together with the ghastly things half hinted in this revealing story purporting to be only *fiction,* opens up a vista of undreamed horror, of age-old evil."

"Good Heaven!" I exclaimed involuntarily. "Surely you can't think this fantasy has come to life?"

Tuttle turned and gave me a strangely distant look. "What *I* think doesn't matter, Haddon," he replied gravely. "But there is one thing I would like very much to know—what happened at *Innsmouth?* What has happened there for decades past that people have shunned it so? Why has this once prosperous port sunk into oblivion, half its houses empty, its property practically worthless? And why was it necessary for Government men to blow up row after row of the waterfront dwellings and warehouses? Lastly, for what earthly reason did they send a submarine to torpedo the marine spaces beyond Devil Reef just out of Innsmouth?"

"I know nothing of that," I replied.

But he paid no heed; his voice rose a little, uncertain and trembling, and he said, "I can tell you, Haddon. It is even as my Uncle Amos has written: Great Cthulhu has risen again!"

For a moment I was shaken; then I said, "But it is Hastur for whom he waited."

"Precisely," agreed Tuttle in a clipped, professorial voice. "Then I should like to know who or what it is that walks in the earth in the dark hours when Fomalhaut has risen and the Hyades are in the east!"

3

With this, he abruptly changed the subject; he began to ask me questions about myself and my practice, and presently, when I rose to go, he asked me to stay the night. This I consented finally, and with some reluctance, to do, whereupon he departed at once to make a room ready for me. I took the opportunity thus afforded to examine his desk more closely for the *Necronomicon* missing from the library of Miskatonic University. It was not on his desk, but, crossing to the shelves, I found it there. I had just taken it down and was examining it to make certain of its identity, when Tuttle reëntered the room. His quick eyes darted to the book in my hands, and he half smiled.

"I wish you'd take that back to Doctor Llanfer when you go in the morning, Haddon," he said casually. "Now that I've copied the text, I have no further use for it."

"I'll do that gladly," I said, relieved that the matter could so easily be settled.

Shortly after, I retired to the room on the second floor which he had prepared for me. He accompanied me as far as the door, and there paused briefly, uncertain of speech ready for his tongue and yet not permitted to pass his lips; for he turned once or twice, bade me goodnight before he spoke what weighed upon his thoughts: "By the way—if you hear anything in the night, don't be alarmed, Haddon. Whatever it is, it's harmless —as yet."

It was not until he had gone and I was alone in my room that the significance of what he had said and the way he had said it dawned upon me. It grew upon me then that this was confirmation of the wild rumors that had penetrated Arkham, and that Tuttle spoke not entirely without fear. I undressed slowly and thoughtfully, and got into the pajamas Tuttle had laid out for me, without deviating for an instant from the pre-occupation with the weird mythology of Amos Tuttle's ancient books that held my mind. Never quick to pass judgment, I was not prone to do so now; despite the apparent absurdity of the structure, it was still sufficiently well erected to merit more than a casual scrutiny. And it was clear to me that Tuttle was more than half convinced of its truth. This in itself was more than enough to give me pause, for Paul Tuttle had distinguished himself time and again for the thoroughness of his researches, and his published papers had not been challenged for even their most minor detail. As a result of facing these facts, I was pre-pared to admit at least that there was some basis for the mythology-structure outlined to me by Tuttle, but as to its truth or error, of course I was in no position at that time to commit myself even within the confines of my own mind; for once a man concedes or condemns a thing within his mind, it is doubly, nay triply, difficult to rid himself of his conclusion, however ill-advised it may subsequently prove to be.

Thinking thus, I got into bed, and lay there awaiting sleep. The night had deepened and darkened, though I could see through the flimsy curtain at the window that the stars were out, Andromeda high in the east, and the constellations of autumn beginning to mount the sky.

I was on the edge of sleep when I was startled awake again by a sound which had been present for some time, but which had only just then been borne in upon me with all its signifi-cance: the faintly trembling step of some gigantic creature

vibrating all through the house, though the sound of it came
not from within the house, but from the east, and for a con-
fused moment I thought of something risen from the sea and
walking along the shore in the wet sand.

But this illusion passed when I raised myself on one elbow
and listened more intently. For a moment there was no sound
whatever; then it came again, irregularly, broken—a step, a
pause, two steps in fairly quick succession, an odd *sucking*
noise. Disturbed, I got up and went to the open window. The
night was warm, and the still air almost sultry; far to the north-
east a beacon cut an arc upon the sky, and from the distant
north came the faint drone of a night plane. It was already
past midnight; low in the east shone red Aldebaran and the
Pleiades, but I did not at that time, as I did later, connect the
disturbances I heard to the appearance of the Hyades above the
horizon.

The odd sounds, meanwhile, continued unabated, and it was
borne in upon me presently that they were indeed approaching
the house, however slow their progress. And that they came
from the direction of the sea I could not doubt, for in this place
there were no configurations of the earth that might have
thrown any sound out of directional focus. I began to think
again of those similar sounds we had heard while Amos Tuttle's
body lay in the house, though I did not then remember that even
as the Hyades lay now low in the east, so they were then setting
in the west. If there were any difference in the manner of their
approach, I was not able to ascertain it, unless it was that the
present disturbances seemed somehow *closer,* but it was not a
physical closeness as much as a psychic *closeness.* The conviction of this was so strong that I began to feel a growing

uneasiness not untinged with fear; I began to experience a wild restlessness, a desire for company; and I went quickly to the door of my room, opened it, and stepped quietly into the hall in search of my host.

But now at once a new discovery made itself known. As long as I had been in my room, the sounds I had heard seemed unquestionably to come from the east, notwithstanding the faint, almost intangible tremors that seemed to shudder through the old house; but here in the darkness of the hall, whither I had gone without a light of any kind, I became aware that the sounds and tremblings alike emanated from *below*—not, indeed, from any place in the house, but below that—rising as if from subterranean places. My nervous tension increased, and I stood uneasily to get my bearings in the dark, when I perceived from the direction of the stairway a faint radiance mounting from below. I moved toward it at once, noiselessly, and, looking over the banister, saw that the light came from an electric candle held in Paul Tuttle's hand. He was standing in the lower hall, clad in his dressing-gown, though it was clear to me even from where I stood that he had not removed his clothes. The light that fell upon his face revealed the intensity of his attention; his head was cocked a little to one side in an attitude of listening, and he stood motionless the while I looked down upon him.

"Paul!" I called in a harsh whisper.

He looked up instantly and saw my face doubtless caught in the light from the candle in his hand. "Do you hear?" he asked.

"Yes—what in God's name it is?"

"I've heard it before," he said. "Come down."

I went down to the lower hall, where I stood for a moment under his penetrating and questioning gaze.

"You aren't afraid, Haddon?"

I shook my head.

"Then come with me."

He turned and led the way toward the back of the house, where he descended into the cellars below. All this time the sounds were rising in volume; it was as if they had approached closer to the house, indeed, almost as if they were directly below, and now there was obvious a definite trembling in the building, not alone of the walls and supports, but one with the shuddering and shaking of the earth all around: it was as if some deep subterranean disturbance had chosen this spot in the earth's surface to make itself manifest. But Tuttle was unmoved by this, doubtless for the reason that he had experienced it before. He went directly through the first and second cellars to a third, set somewhat lower than the others, and apparently of more recent construction, but, like the first two, built of limestone blocks set in cement.

In the center of this sub-cellar he paused and stood quietly listening. The sounds had by this time risen to such intensity that it seemed as if the house were caught in a vortex of volcanic upheaval without actually suffering the destruction of its supports; for the trembling and shuddering, the creaking and groaning of the rafters above us gave evidence of the tremendous pressure exerted within the earth beneath us, and even the stone floor of the cellar seemed alive under my bare feet. But presently these sounds appeared to recede into the background, though actually they lessened not at all, and only presented this illusion because of our growing familiarity with them and because our ears were becoming attuned to other sounds in more major keys, these, too, rising from below as from a great distance, but carrying with them an insidious hellishness in the implications that grew upon us.

For the first whistling sounds were not clear enough to justify any guess as to their origin, and it was not until I had been listening for some time that it occurred to me that the sounds breaking into the weird whistling or whimpering derived from something alive, some sentient being, for presently they resolved into uncouth and shocking mouthings, indistinct and not intelligible even when they could be clearly heard. By this time, Tuttle had put the candle down, had come to his knees, and now half lay upon the floor with his ear close to the stone.

In obedience to his motion, I did likewise, and found that the sounds from below resolved into more recognizable syllables, though no less meaningless. For the first while, I heard nothing but incoherent and apparently unconnected ululations, with which were interpolated chanting sounds, which later I put down as follows: *Iä! Iä! . . . Shub-Niggurath. . . . Ugh! Cthulhu fhtagn! . . . Iä! Iä! Cthulhu!*

But that I was in some error in regard to at least one of these sounds, I soon learned. *Cthulhu* itself was plainly audible, despite the fury of mounting sound all around; but the word that followed now seemed somewhat longer than *fhtagn;* it was as if an extra syllable had been added, and yet I could not be certain that it had not been there all the while, for presently it came clearer, and Tuttle took from a pocket his notebook and pencil and wrote:

"They are saying *Cthulhu naflfhtagn.*"

Judging by the expression of his eyes, faintly elated, this

evidently conveyed something to him, but to me it meant nothing, apart from my ability to recognize a portion of it as identical in character with the words that appeared in the abhorred *R'lyeh Text,* and subsequently again in the magazine story, where its translation would seem to have indicated that the words meant: *Cthulhu waits dreaming.* My obvious blank ignorance of his meaning apparently recalled to my host that his philological learning was far in excess of mine, for he smiled bleakly and whispered, "It can be nothing else but a negative construction."

Even then I did not at once understand that he meant to explain that the subterranean voices were not saying what I had thought, but: *Cthulhu no longer waits dreaming!* There was now no longer any question of belief, for the things that were taking place were of no human origin, and admitted of no other solution than one in some way, however remotely, related to the incredible mythology Tuttle had so recently expounded to me. And now, as if this evidence of feeling and hearing were not enough, there became manifest a strange fetid smell mingled with a nauseatingly strong odor of fish, apparently seeping up through the porous limestone.

Tuttle became aware of this almost simultaneously with my own recognition, and I was alarmed to observe in his features traces of apprehension stronger than any I had heretofore noticed. He lay for a moment quietly; then he rose stealthily, took up the candle, and crept from the room, beckoning me after him.

Only when we were once more on the upper story did he venture to speak. "They are closer than I thought," he said then, musingly.

"Is it Hastur?" I asked nervously.

But he shook his head. "It cannot be he, because the passage below leads only to the sea and is doubtless partly full of water. Therefore it can only be one of the Water Beings—those who took refuge there when the torpedoes destroyed Devil him, as the Mi-Go serve in the icy fastnesses, and the Tcho-Reef beyond shunned Innsmouth—Cthulhu, or those who serve Tcho people serve on the hidden plateaus of Asia."

Since it was impossible to sleep, we sat for a time in the library, while Tuttle spoke in a half-chanting manner of th strange things he had come upon in the old books that had been his uncle's: sat waiting for the dawn while he told of the dreaded Plateau of Leng, of the Black Goat of the Woods with a Thousand Young, of Azathoth and Nyarlathotep, the Mighty Messenger who walked the star-spaces in the semblance of man; of the horrible and diabolic Yellow Sign, the haunted and fabled towers of mysterious Carcosa; of terrible Lloigor and hated Zhar; of Ithaqua the Snow-Thing, of Chaugnar Faugn and N'gha-Kthun, of unknown Kadath and the Fungi from Yuggoth—so he talked for hours while the sounds below continued and I sat listening in a deadly, terror-fraught fear. And yet that fear was needless, for with the dawn the stars paled, and the tumult below died subtly away, fading toward the east and the ocean's deeps, and I went at last to my room, eagerly, to dress in preparation for my leave-taking.

4

In little over a month, I was again on my way to the Tuttle estate, via Arkham, in response to an urgent card from Paul, upon which he had scrawled in a shaky hand the single word: Come! Even if he had not written, I should have considered it my duty to return to the old house on the Aylesbury Road, despite my distaste for Tuttle's soul-shaking research and the now active fear I could not help but feel. Still, I had been holding off ever since coming to the decision that I should attempt to dissuade Tuttle from further research until the morning of the day on which his card came. On that morning I found in the *Transcript* a garbled story from Arkham: I would not have noticed it at all, had it not been for the small head to take the eye: *Outrage in Arkham Cemetery*, and below: *Tuttle Vault Violated*. The story was brief, and disclosed little beyond the information already conveyed by the headings:

> It was discovered here early this morning that vandals had broken into and partly destroyed the Tuttle vault in Arkham cemetery. One wall is smashed almost beyond repair, and the coffins have been disturbed. It has been reported that the coffin of the late Amos Tuttle is missing, but confirmation cannot be had by the time this issue goes to press.

Immediately upon reading this vague bulletin, I was seized with the strongest apprehension, come upon me from I know not what source; yet I felt at once that the outrage perpetrated upon the vault was not an ordinary crime, and I could not help connecting it in my mind with the occurrences at the old Tuttle house. I had therefore resolved to go to Arkham, and thence to see Paul Tuttle, before his card arrived; his brief message alarmed me still more, if possible, and at the same time convinced me of what I feared—that some revolting connection existed between the cemetery outrage and the things that walked in the earth beneath the house on Aylesbury Road. But at the same time I became aware of a deep reluctance to leave Boston, obsessed with an intangible fear of invisible danger from an unknown source. Still, duty compelled my going, and however strongly I might shun it, go I must.

I arrived in Arkham in early afternoon and went at once to the cemetery, in my capacity as solicitor, to ascertain the extent of the damage done. A police guard had been established, but I was permitted to examine the premises as soon as my identity had been disclosed. The newspaper account, I found, had been shockingly inadequate, for the ruin of the Tuttle vault was virtually complete, its coffins exposed to the sun's warmth, some of them broken open, revealing long-dead bones. While it was true that Amos Tuttle's coffin had disappeared in the night, it had been found at midday in an open field about two miles east of Arkham, too far from the road to have been carried there; and the mystery of its being there was, if anything, deeper now than at the time the coffin had been found; for an investigation had disclosed certain deep indentations set at wide intervals in the earth, some of them as much as forty feet in diameter! It was as if some monstrous creature had walked there, though I confess that this thought occurred only within my own mind; the impressions in the earth remained a mystery upon which no light was thrown even by the wildest surmises as to their source. This may have been partly due to the more startling fact that had emerged immediately upon the finding of the coffin: the body of Amos Tuttle had vanished, and a search of the surrounding terrain had failed to disclose it. So much I learned from the custodian of the cemetery before I set out along the Aylesbury Road, refusing to think further about this incredible information until I had spoken with Paul Tuttle.

This time my summons at his door was not immediately

answered, and I had begun to wonder with some apprehension whether something had happened to him, when I detected a faint scuffling sound beyond the door, and almost immediately heard Tuttle's muffled voice.

"Who is it?"

"Haddon," I replied, and heard what seemed to be a gasp of relief.

The door opened, and it was not until it had closed that I became aware of the nocturnal darkness of the hall, and saw that the window at the far end had been tightly shuttered, and that no light fell into the long corridor from any of the rooms opening off it. I forebore to ask the question that came to my tongue and turned instead to Tuttle. It was some time before my eyes had mastered the unnatural darkness sufficiently to make him out, and then I was conscious of a distinct feeling of shock; for Tuttle had changed from a tall, upright man in his prime to a bent, heavy man of uncouth and faintly repulsive appearance, betraying an age which actually was not his. And his first words filled me with high alarm.

"Quick now, Haddon," he said. "There's not much time."

"What is it? What's wrong, Paul?" I asked.

He disregarded this, leading the way into the library, where an electric candle burned dimly. "I've made a packet of some of my uncle's most valuable books—the *R'lyeh Text, The Book of Eibon,* the *Pnakotic Manuscripts*—some others. These must go to the library of Miskatonic University by your hand today without fail. They are henceforth to be considered the property of the library. And here is an envelope containing certain instructions to you, in case I fail to get in touch with you either personally or by telephone—which I have had installed here since your last visit—by ten o'clock tonight. You are staying, I assume, at the Lewiston House. Now attend me closely: if I fail to telephone you to the contrary before ten o'clock tonight, you are to follow the instructions herein contained without hesitation. I advise you to act immediately, and, since you may feel them too unusual to proceed swiftly, I have already telephoned Judge Wilton and explained that I've left some strange but vital instructions with you, but that I want them carried out to the letter."

"What's happened, Paul?" I asked.

For a moment it seemed as if he would speak freely, but he only shook his head and said, "As yet I do not know all. But this much I can say: we have both, my uncle and I, made a terrible mistake. And I fear it is now too late to rectify it. You have learned of the disappearance of Uncle Amos's body?"

I nodded.

"It has since turned up."

I was astounded, since I had only just come from Arkham, and no such intelligence had been imparted to me. "Impossible!" I exclaimed. "They are still searching."

"Ah, no matter," he said oddly. "It is not there. It is here—at the foot of the garden, where it was abandoned when it was found useless."

At this, he jerked his head up suddenly, and we heard the shuffling and grunting sound that came from somewhere in the house. But in a moment it died away, and he turned again to me.

"The haven," he muttered, and gave a sickly laugh. "The tunnel was built by Uncle Amos, I am sure. But it was not the haven Hastur wanted—though it serves the minions of his half-brother, Great Cthulhu."

It was almost impossible to realize that the sun shone outside, for the murkiness of the room and the atmosphere of impending dread that hung over me combined to lend to the scene an unreality apart from the world from which I had just come, despite the horror of the violated vault. I perceived also about Tuttle an air of almost feverish expectancy coupled with a nervous haste; his eyes shone oddly and seemed more prominent than I had previously known them, his lips seemed to have coarsened and thickened, and his beard had become matted to a degree I would not have thought possible. He listened now only for a moment before he turned back to me.

"I myself need to stay for the present; I have not finished mining the place, and that must be done," he resumed erractically, but went on before the questions that rose in me could find utterance. "I've discovered that the house rests upon a natural artificial foundation, that below the place there must be not only the tunnel, but a mass of cavernous structures, and I believe that these caverns are for the most part water-filled—and perhaps inhabited," he added as a sinister afterthought. "But this, of course, is at the present time of small importance. I have no immediate fear of what is below, but what I know is to come."

Once again he paused to listen, and again vague, distant sounds came to our ears. I listened intently, hearing an ominous fumbling, as if some creature were trying a door, and strove to discover or guess at its origin. I had thought at first that the sound emanated from somewhere within the house, thought almost instinctively of the attic; for it seemed to come from above, but in a moment it was borne in upon me that the sound did not derive from any place within the house, nor yet from any portion of the house outside, but grew from some place beyond that, from *a point in space beyond the walls of the house* —a fumbling, plucking noise which was not associated in my consciousness with any recognizable material sounds, but was rather an unearthly invasion. I peered at Tuttle, and saw that his attention was also for something from outside, for his head was somewhat lifted and his eyes looked beyond the enclosing walls, bearing in them a curiously rapt expression, not without fear, nor yet without a strange air of helpless waiting.

"That is Hastur's sign," he said in a hushed voice. "When the Hyades rise and Aldebaran stalks the sky tonight, He will come. The Other will be here with His water people, those of the primal gilled races." Then he began to laugh suddenly, soundlessly, and with a sly, half-mad glance, added, "And Cthulhu and Hastur shall struggle here for the haven while Great Orion strides above the horizon, with Betelguese where the Elder Gods are, who alone can block the evil designs of these hellish spawn!"

My astonishment at his words doubtless showed in my face and in turn made him understand what shocked hesitation and doubt I felt, for abruptly his expression altered, his eyes softened, his hands clasped and unclasped nervously, and his voice became more natural.

"But perhaps this tires you, Haddon," he said. "I will say no more, for the time grows short, the evening approaches, and in a little while the night. I beg you to have no question about following the instructions I have outlined in this brief note for your eyes. I charge you to follow my directions implicitly. If it is as I fear, even that may be of no avail; if it is not, I shall reach you in time."

With that he picked up the packet of books, placed it in my hands, and led me to the door, whither I followed him without protest, for I was bewildered and not a little unmanned at the strangeness of his actions, the uncanny atmosphere of brooding horror that clung to the ancient, menace-ridden house.

At the threshold he paused briefly and touched my arm lightly. "Goodbye, Haddon," he said with friendly intensity.

Then I found myself on the stoop in the glare of the lowering sunlight so bright that I closed my eyes against it until I could again accustom myself to its brilliance, while the cheerful chortle of a late bluebird on a fence-post across the road sounded pleasantly in my ears, as if to belie the atmosphere of dark fear and eldritch horror behind.

5

I come now to that portion of my narrative upon which I am loath to embark, not alone because of the incredibility of what I must write, but because it can at best be a vague, uncertain account, replete with surmises and remarkable, if disjointed, evidence of horror-torn, eon-old evil beyond time, of primal things that lurk just outside the pale of life we know, or terrible, animate survival in the hidden places of Earth. How much of this Tuttle learned from those hellish texts he entrusted to my care for the locked shelves of Miskatonic University Library, I cannot say. Certain it is that he guessed many things he did not know until too late; of others, he gathered hints, though it is to be doubted that he fully comprehended the magnitude of the task upon which he so thoughtlessly embarked when he sought to learn why Amos Tuttle had willed the deliberate destruction of his house and books.

Following my return to Arkham's ancient streets, events succeeded events with undesirable rapidity. I deposited Tuttle's packet of books with Doctor Llanfer at the library, and made my way immediately after to Judge Wilton's house, where I was fortunate enough to find him. He was just sitting down to supper, and invited me to join him, which I did, though I had no appetite of any kind, indeed, food seeming repugnant to me. By this time all the fears and intangible doubts I had held had come to a head within me, and Wilton saw at once that I was laboring under an unusual nervous strain.

"Curious thing about the Tuttle vault, isn't it?" he ventured shrewdly, guessing at the reason for my presence in Arkham.

"Yes, but not half so curious as the circumstance of Amos Tuttle's body reposing at the foot of his garden," I replied.

"Indeed," said he without any visible sign of interest, his calmness serving to restore me in some measure to a sense of tranquillity. "I dare say you've come from there and know whereof you speak."

At that, I told him as briefly as possible the story I had come to tell, omitting only a few of the more improbable details, but not entirely succeeding in dismissing his doubts, though he was far too much a gentleman to permit me to feel them. He sat for a while in thoughtful silence after I had finished, glancing once or twice at the clock, which showed the hour to be already past seven. Presently he interrupted his revery to suggest that I telephone the Lewiston House and arrange for any call for me to be transferred to Judge Wilton's home. This I did instantly,

somewhat relieved that he had consented to take the problem
seriously enough to devote his evening to it.

"As for the mythology," he said, directly upon my return to
the room, "it *can be* dismissed as the creation of a mad mind,
the Arab Abdul Alhazred. I say advisedly, it *can be,* but in the
light of the things which have happened in Innsmouth I should
not like to commit myself. However, we are not at present in
session. The immediate concern is for Paul Tuttle himself; I
propose that we examine his instructions to you forthwith."

I produced the envelope at once, and opened it. It contained
but a single sheet of paper, bearing these cryptic and ominous
lines:

"I have mined the house and all. Go *immediately* without delay, to the pasture gate west of the house, where in the shrubbery on the right side of the lane as you approach from Arkham, I have concealed the detonator. My Uncle Amos was
right—it should have been done in the first place. If you fail
me, Haddon, then before God you loose upon the countryside
such a scourge as man has never known and will never see again
—if indeed he survives it!"

Some inkling of the cataclysmic truth must at that moment
have begun to penetrate my mind, for when Judge Wilton
leaned back, looked at me quizzically, and asked, "What are
you going to do?" I replied without hesitation: "I'm going to
follow those instructions to the letter!"

He gazed at me for a moment without comment; then he
bowed to the inevitable and settled back. "We shall wait for ten
o'clock together," he said gravely.

The final act of the incredible horror that had its focal point
in the Tuttle house took place just a little before ten, coming

upon us in the beginning in so disarmingly prosaic a manner that the full horror, when it came, was doubly shocking and profound. For at five minutes to ten, the telephone rang. Judge Wilton took it at once, and even from where I sat I could hear the agonized voice of Paul Tuttle calling my name.

I took the telephone from Judge Wilton.

"This is Haddon," I said with a calmness I did not feel. "What is it, Paul?"

"Do it now!" he cried. "Oh, God, Haddon—right away—before . . . too late. Oh, God—the haven! *The haven!* . . . You know the place . . . pasture gate. O, God, be quick! . . ." And then there happened what I shall never forget: the sudden, terrible degeneration of his voice, so that it was as if it crumpled together and sank into abysmal mouthings; for the sounds that care over the wire were bestial and inhuman—shocking gibberings and crude, brutish, drooling sounds, from among which certain of them recurred again and again, and I listened in steadily mounting horror to the triumphant gibbering before it died away:

"Iä! Iä! Hastur! Ugh! Ugh! Iä Hastur cf'ayak 'vulgtmm, vugtlagln vulgtmm! Ai! Shub-Niggurath! . . . Hastur—Hastur cf'tagn! Iä! Iä! Hastur! . . ."

Then abruptly all sound died away, and I turned to face Judge Wilton's terror-stricken features. And yet I did not see him, nor did I see anything in my understanding of what must be done; for abruptly, with cataclysmic effect, I understood what Tuttle had failed to know until too late. And at once I dropped the telephone; at once I ran hatless and coatless from the house into the street, with the sound of Judge Wilton frantically summoning police over the telephone fading into the

night behind me. I ran with unnatural speed from the shad-
owed, haunted streets of witch-cursed Arkham into the October
night, down the Aylesbury Road, into the lane and the pasture
gate, where for one brief instant, while sirens blew behind me,
I saw the Tuttle house through the orchard outlined in a hellish
purple glow, beautiful but unearthly and tangibly evil.

Then I pushed down the detonator, and with a tremendous
roar, the old house burst asunder and flames leaped up where
the house had stood.

For a few dazed moments I stood there, aware suddenly of
the arrival of police along the road south of the house, before
I began to move up to join them, and so saw that the explosion
had brought about what Paul Tuttle had hinted: the collapse of
the subterranean caverns below the house; for the land itself
was settling, slipping down, and the flames that had risen were
hissing and steaming in the water gushing up from below.

Then it was that that other thing happened—the last unearthly horror that mercifully blotted out what I saw in the
wreckage jutting out above the rising waters—the great protoplasmic mass risen from the center of the lake forming where
the Tuttle house had been, and the thing that came crying out
at us across the lawn before it turned to face that other and begin a titanic struggle for mastery interrupted only by the brilliant explosion of light that seemed to emanate from the eastern
sky like a bolt of incredibly powerful lightning; a tremendous
discharge of energy in the shape of light, so that for one awful
moment everything was revealed—before lightning-like appendages descended as from the heart of the blinding pillar of
light itself, one seizing the mass in the waters, lifting it high,
and casting it far out to sea, the other taking that second thing

from the lawn and hurling it, a dark dwindling blot, into the sky, where it vanished among the eternal stars! And then came sudden, absolute, cosmic silence, and where, a moment before, this miracle of light had been, there was now only darkness and the line of trees against the sky, and low in the east the gleaming eye of Betelguese as Orion rose into the autumn night.

For an instant I did not know which was worse—the chaos of the previous moment, or the utter black silence of the present; but the small cries of horrified men brought it back to me, and it was borne in upon me then that they at least did not understand the secret horror, the final thing that sears and maddens, the thing that rises in the dark hours to stalk the bottomless depths of the mind. They may have heard, as I did, that thin, far, whistling sound, that maddening ululation from the deep, immeasurable gulf of cosmic space, the wailing that fell back along the wind, and the syllables that floated down the slopes of air: *Tekeli-li, tekeli-li, tekeli-li* . . . And certainly they saw the thing that came crying out at us from the sinking ruins behind, the distorted caricature of a human being, with its eyes sunk to invisibility in thick masses of scaly flesh, the thing that flailed its arms bonelessly at us like the appendages of an octopus, *the thing that shrieked and gibbered in Paul Tuttle's voice!*

But they could not know the secret that I alone knew, the secret Amos Tuttle might have guessed in the shadows of his dying hours, the thing Paul Tuttle was too late in learning: *that the haven sought by Hastur the Unspeakable, the haven promised Him Who is not to be Named, was not the tunnel, and not the house, but the body and soul of Amos Tuttle himself, and, failing these, the living flesh and immortal soul of him who lived in that doomed house on the Aylesbury Road!*

The Whippoorwills in the Hills

I TOOK POSSESSION of my cousin Abel Harrop's house on the last day of April, 1928, because it was plain by that time that the men from the sheriff's office at Aylesbury were either unable or unwilling to make any progress in explaining his disappearance, and I was determined therefore to carry on my own investigation. This was a matter of principle, rather than of affection, for my cousin Abel had always been somewhat apart from the rest of the family; he had had a reputation since his adolescene for being queer and had never made any effort to visit the rest of us or to invite our own visits. Nor was his plain house in a remote valley seven miles off the Aylesbury Pike out of Arkham particularly a place to excite interest in most of us, who lived in Boston and Portland. I especially want this to be clear, since subsequent events make it imperative that no other motive be ascribed to my coming to stay in the house.

My cousin Abel's home was, as I have said, very plain. It was built in the conventional fashion of New England houses, many of which can be seen in scores of villages throughout and even farther south; it was a kind of rectangular house, of two storeys, with a stoop out back and a front porch set in one corner in order to complete the rectangle. This porch had at one time been efficiently screened, but there were now small tears in the screen, and it presented a general air of decay. However, the house itself, which was of wood, was neat enough; its siding had been painted white less than a year ago before my cousin's disappearance, and this coat of paint had worn well enough so that the house seemed quite new, as apart from the screened porch. There was a woodshed off to the right, and a smokehouse near that. There was also an open well, with a roof over it, and a windlass with buckets on it. On the left there was another, more serviceable pump, and two smaller sheds. As my cousin did not farm, there was no place for animals.

The interior of the house was in good condition. Clearly, my cousin had always kept it well, though the furnishings were somewhat worn and faded, having been inherited from his parents, who had died two decades before. The lower floor consisted of a small, confining kitchen which opened to the stoop out back, an old-fashioned parlor, somewhat larger than most, and a room which had evidently once been a dining-room, but which had been converted into a study by my cousin Abel, and was filled with books—on crude, home-made shelves, on boxes, chairs, a secretary and the table. There were even piles of them on the floor, and one book lay open on the table, just as it had lain when my cousin disappeared; they had told me at the courthouse in Aylesbury that nothing had been disturbed. The second storey was a gable storey; its rooms all had sloping roofs, though there were three of them, all small, two of which were bedrooms, and the third a store-room. Each room had one gable-window, no more. One of the bedrooms was over the kitchen, one over the parlor, and the store-room was over the study. There was no reason to believe that my cousin Abel had occupied either of the bedrooms, however; indications were that he made use of a couch in the parlor, and, since the couch was softer than usual, I determined to use it also. The stairway to the second floor led up out of the kitchen, thereby contributing to the lack of room.

The events of my cousin's disappearance were very simple, as any reader who may remember the spare newspaper accounts can testify. He had last been seen in Aylesbury early in April; he had bought five pounds of coffee, ten pounds of sugar, some wire, and a large amount of netting. Four days afterward, on the seventh of April, a neighbor, passing by and failing to observe smoke coming from the chimney, went in, after some reluctance; my cousin had apparently not been very well liked; having a surly nature, and his neighbors had kept away from him, but, since the seventh was a cold day, Lem Giles had gone up to the door and rapped. When there was no answer, he pushed on the door; it was open and he went in. He found the house deserted and cold, and a lamp which had been used beside a book still open on the table had plainly burned itself out. While Giles thought this a curious state of affairs, he did not report it until three days after that, on the tenth, when he again passed by the house on his way to Aylesbury, and, stopping for a similar reason, found nothing altered in any way in the house. At that time he spoke to a store-keeper in Aylesbury about it and was advised to report the matter at the sheriff's office. With great reluctance, he did so. A deputy-sheriff drove out to my cousin's place and looked around. Since there had been a thaw, there was nothing to show footprints, the snow having been quickly melted away. And since a little of the coffee and sugar my cousin had bought had been used, it was assumed that he had vanished within a day or so of his visit to Aylesbury. There was some evidence—as there still was in the loose pile of netting in a rocking-chair in one corner of the parlor—that my cousin was planning to do something with the netting he had bought; but, since it was of the type used in seines along the coast at Kingsport for the purpose of catching rough fish, his intention was obscured in some mystery.

The efforts of the sheriff's men from Aylesbury were, as I have hinted, only perfunctory. There was nothing to show that they were eager to investigate Abel's disappearance; perhaps they were too readily discouraged by the reticence of his neighbors. I did not mean to be. If the reports of the sheriff's men were reliable—and I had no reason to believe they were not—then his neighbors had steadfastly avoided Abel and even now, after his disappearance, when he was presumed dead, they were no more willing to speak of him than they had been to associate with him before. Indeed, I had tangible evidence of the neighbor's feeling before I had been in my cousin's house a day.

Though the house was not wired for electric lights, it was on a telephone line. When the telephone rang in mid-afternoon —less than two hours after my arrival at the house—I went over and took the receiver off the hook, forgetting that my cousin was on a party line. I had been dilatory to answer, and when I removed the receiver, someone was already talking. Even then, I would have replaced the receiver without more ado, had it not been for mention of my cousin's name. Being possessed of a natural share of curiosity, I stood still, listening.

". . . somebody's come to Abe Harrop's house," came a woman's voice. "Lem come by there from town ten minutes ago and seen it."

Ten minutes, I thought. That would be Lem Giles' place, the nearest neighbor up the Pocket and over the hill.

"Oh, Mis' Giles, ye don't s'pose *he's* come back?"

"Hope the Lord he don't! But 'tain't *him*. Leastwise, Lem said it didn't look like him nohow."

"If *he* comes back, I want to git aout o' here. There's been enough goin's-on for a decent body."

"They ain't found hide nor hair of *him*."

"An' they wun't, neither. *They* got him. I knowed he was a-callin' 'em. Amos told him right off to git rid o' them books, but he knowed better. A-settin' there night after night, readin' in them devilish books."

"Don't you worry none, Hester."

"All these goin's-on, it's a God's mercy a body's alive to worry!"

This somewhat ambiguous conversation convinced me that the natives of this secluded Pocket of hill country knew far more than they had told the men from the sheriff's office. But this initial conversation was only the beginning. Thereafter the telephone rang at half-hour intervals, and my arrival at my cousin's house was the principal topic of conversation. Thereafter, too, I listened shamelessly.

The neighbors circling the Pocket where the house stood numbered seven families, none of which was in sight of any part of my cousin's house. There were, in this order: up the pocket, Lem and Abby Giles, and their two sons, Arthur and Albert, with one daughter, Virginia, a feeble-minded girl in her late twenties; beyond them, well up into the next Pocket, Lute and Jethro Corey, bachelors, with a hired man, Curtis Begbie; east of them, deep in the hills, Seth Whateley, his wife, Emma, and their three children, Willie, Mamie, and Ella; down from them, and opposite my cousin's house about a mile to the east, Laban Hough, a widower, his children, Susie and Peter, and his sister, Lavinia; about a half mile further down, along the road that led into the Pocket, Clem Osborn and his wife, Marie, with two hired men, John and Andrew Baxter; and finally, over the hills west of my cousin's house, Rufus and Angeline Wheeler, with their sons, Perry and Nathaniel and the three spinster Hutchins sisters, Hester, Josephine, and Amelia, with two hired men, Jesse Trumbull and Amos Whateley.

All these people were connected to the single party line which included my cousin's telephone. In the course of three hours, what with one woman calling another, back and forth without any end before supper-time, everyone on the line had been informed of my coming, and, as each woman added her bit of information, each of the others learned who I was, and correctly guessed my purpose. All this was perhaps natural enough in such isolated neighborhoods, where the most trivial event is a subject of deep concern to people who have little else to engage their attention; but what was disturbing about this fire of gossip on the party wire was the unmistakable undercurrent of fear which was omnipresent. Clearly, my cousin Abel Harrop had been shunned for some reason connected with this incredible fear of him and whatever it was he was doing. It was sobering to reflect that out of such primitive fear could very easily rise the decision to kill in order to escape that fear.

I knew it would be no easy task to break down the suspicious reserve of the neighbors, but I was determined that it must and would be done. I retired early that night, but I did not reckon with the difficulties of going to sleep in such an environment as my cousin's house. Where I had expected an unbroken silence, I found instead a maddening cacophony of sound which assaulted and engulfed the house. Beginning a half hour after sundown, in mid-twilight, there was such a calling of whippoorwills as I have never heard before; where one bird had called alone for five minutes or thereabouts, in thirty minutes there were twenty birds calling, and in an hour the number of whippoorwills seemed to have risen to well over a hundred. Moreover, the configuration of the Pocket was such that the hills at one side threw back the echoes of sounds from the other, so that the voices of a hundred birds soon assumed the proportions of two, varying in intensity from a demanding scream rising with explosive force from just beyond my window to a faintly whispered call coming from far up or down the valley. Knowing a little of the habits of whippoorwills, I fully expected the calls to cease within an hour of beginning, and to start up again just before dawn. In this I was mistaken. Not only did the birds call incessantly all night long, but it was unmistakably evident that a large number of them flew in from the woods to sit on the roof of the house, as well as on the sheds and the ground around the house, making such a deafening racket that I was completely unable to sleep until dawn, when, one by one, they drifted away and were silent.

I knew then that I could not long withstand this nerve-wracking cacophony of song.

I had not slept an hour before I was awakened, still exhausted, by the ringing of the telephone. I got up and took down the receiver, wondering what was wanted at this hour, and who was calling. I muttered a sleepy, "Hello."

"Harrop?"

"This is Dan Harrop," I said.

"Got suthin' to tell ye. Air ye listenin'?"

"Who is this?" I asked.

"Listen t' me, Harrop. If you knows what's good fer ye, ye'll git aout o' there as fast as ye c'n git!"

Before I could register my astonishment, the line went dead. I was still somewhat drowsy from lack of sleep. I stood for a moment; then hung up the receiver. A man's voice, gruff and old. Certainly one of the neighbors; the telephone bell had rung as if it had been ground by someone on the line and not by the central.

I was half way back to my makeshift bed in the parlor when the telephone rang again. Though it was not my ring, I turned back to it at once. The hour was now six-thirty, and the sun shone over the hill. It was Emma Whateley calling Lavinia Hough.

"Vinnie, did ye hear 'em las' night?"

"Land sakes, yes! Emma, do you s'pose it means . . .?"

"I don't know. It was suthin' turrible the way they went on. Ain't heerd nuthin' like it since Abel was aout in the woods las' summer. Kept Willie and Mamie awake all night. It scares me, Vinnie."

"Me, too. Gawd, what if it starts again?"

"Hush up, Vinnie. A body can't tell who's listenin'."

The telephone rang throughout the morning, and this was the topic of conversation. It was soon borne in upon me that it was the whippoorwills and their frenetic calling in the night which had excited the neighbors. I had thought it annoying, but it had not occurred to me to think it unusual. However, judging by what I overheard, it was not only unusual but ominous for the birds to call with such insistence. It was Hester Hutchins who put the superstitious fears of the neighbors into words, when she told about the whippoorwills to a cousin who had telephoned from Dunwich, some miles to the north.

"The hills was a'talkin' again las' night, Cousin Flora," she said in a kind of hushed but urgent voice. "Heard 'em all night long, couldn't hardly sleep. Warn't nuthin' but whippoorwills, hundreds an' hundreds of 'em all night long. Come from Harrop's Pocket, but they was so loud they might's well 've been on the porch rail. They're a-waitin' to ketch somebody's soul, just the way they was when Benjy Wheeler died an' sister Hough, an' Curtis Begbie's wife, Annie. I know, I know—they dun't fool me none. Somebody's a-goin' to die—an' soon, mark my words."

A strange superstition, surely, I thought. Nevertheless, that night, following a day too busy to permit of my making inquiries of the neighbors, I set myself to listening for the whippoorwills. I sat in the darkness at the study window, but there was scarcely any need for light, for a moon but three days from the full shone into the valley and filled it with that green-white light which is the peculiar property of moonlight. Long before darkness came into the valley, it had taken possession of the wooded hills enclosing it; and it was from the dark places in the woods that the first steady *whippoorwill* began to sound and recur. Previous to the voices of the whippoorwills there had been strangely few of the customary evening songs of birds; only a few nighthawks had appeared against the evening sky to spiral upward, crying shrilly, and plummet down in a breathtaking sky-coast, making an odd *zoom* at the trough of the dive. But these were no longer visible or audible as darkness fell, and one after another, the whippoorwills began to call.

As darkness invaded the valley, the whippoorwills did likewise. Undeniably, the whippoorwills drifted down out of the hills on noiseless wings toward the house in which I sat. I saw the first one come, a dark object in the moonlight, to the roof of the wood-shed; in a matter of moments, another bird followed, then another and another. Soon I saw them come to the ground between the sheds and the house, and I knew they were on the roof of the house itself. They occupied every roof, every fence-post. I counted over a hundred of them before I stopped counting, being unsure about their flight-patterns, since I observed some of them moving about from one place to another.

Never once did their calling cease. I used to think that the call of the whippoorwill was a sweetly nostalgic sound, but never again. Surrounding the house, the birds made the most hellish cacophony conceivable; whereas the call of a whippoorwill heard from a distance is mellow and pleasant, the same call heard just outside the window is unbelievably harsh and noisy, a cross between a scream and an angry rattle. Multiplied by scores, the calls were truly maddening, grating on me to such an extent that after an hour of it, following the ordeal of the previous night, I took refuge in cotton stuffed into my ears. Even this afforded but temporary relief, but, with its help and the exhaustion I felt after the sleepless night just past, I was able to sleep after a fashion. My last thought before sleep overcame me was that I must go on about my business without delay, lest I be driven out of my mind by the ceaseless insistence of the whippoorwills which obviously meant to come down out of the hills every night in their season.

I was awake before dawn; the soporific of sleep had worn off, but the whippoorwills had not ceased to call. I sat up on my couch, and presently got up to look out of the window. The birds were still there, though they had moved a little farther away from the house now, and were no longer quite so numerous. A faint hint of dawn shone in the east, and there, too, taking the place of the moon, which had gone down, shone the morning stars—the planets Mars, already well up the eastern heaven, with Venus and Jupiter, less than five degrees above the eastern rim, and glowing with supernal splendor.

I dressed, made myself some breakfast, and for the first time stopped to look at the books my cousin Abel had gathered together. I had given a cursory glance at the open book on the table, but it meant nothing to me, since it appeared to be printed in a type-face which was an imitation of someone's script, and was therefore scarcely legible. Moreover, it concerned alien matters, which seemed to me the veriest fancies of somone's drug-ridden mind. My cousin's other books, however, appeared to be of similar nature. A file of the *Old Farmer's Almanac* stood out with welcome familiarity, but this alone was familiar. Though I was never a poorly-read man, I confess to a feeling of utter strangeness before my cousin's library, if such it can be called.

Yet a cursory examination of it filled me with a new respect for my cousin, for his abilities certainly exceeded my own in the matter of languages, if he had been able to read all the tomes he had collected. For they were in several languages, as their titles indicated, and most of them had no meaning for me at all. I remembered having vaguely heard of the Rev. Ward Phillips' book, *Thaumaturgical Prodigies in the New-English Canaan,* but of such books as the *Cultes des Goules,* by Comte d'Erlette, *De Vermis Mysteriis,* by Dr. Ludvig Prinn, Lully's *Ars Magna et Ultima,* the *Pnakotic Manuscript,* the *R'lyeh Text,* Von Junzt's *Unaussprechlichen Kulten,* and many other similar titles, I had never heard. It did not occur to me, frankly, that these books might contain a key to my cousin's disappearance, until later that day, when finally I did take time to make some attempt to see the neighbors, for the purpose of making inquiry among them in the hope of accomplishing more than the men from the sheriff's office.

I went first to the Giles place, which was approximately one mile up into the hills directly south of my cousin's house. My reception was not encouraging. Abbey Giles, a tall, gaunt woman, saw me from the window, shaking her head, refused to come to the door. As I stood in the yard, wondering how I could convince her that I was not dangerous, Lem Giles came hurriedly from the barn; the belligerence of his gaze gave me pause.

"What're ye wantin' here, Stranger?" he asked.

Though he called me "Stranger", I felt that he knew me perfectly well. I introduced myself and explained that I was endeavoring to learn the truth about my cousin's disappearance. Could he tell me anything about Abel?

"Can't tell ye nutin'," he said shortly. "Go ast the sheriff; I tol' him everythin' I got to say."

"I think people hereabouts know more than they are saying," I said firmly.

"Might be. But they ain't sayin' it, and that's a fact."

More than this I could not get out of Lem Giles. I went on

to the Corey place, but no one was at home there; so I took a
ridge path I was confident would lead me to the Hutchins place,
as it did. But before I could get to the house, I was seen from
one of the hill fields, someone hailed me, and I found myself
confronting a barrel-chested man half a head taller than myself, who demanded truculently to know where I was going.

"I'm on my way to Hutchins," I said.

"No need your goin', then," he said. "They ain't to home. I
work for 'em. Name's Amos Whateley."

But I had spoken to Amos Whateley before; I recognized
his voice as that of the man who had early that morning told me
to "git aout o'here as fast as ye c'n git!" I looked at him for a
minute in silence.

"I'm Dan Harrop," I said finally. "I came up here to find out
what happened to my cousin Abel, and I mean to find out."

I could see that he had known who I was. He stood considering me for a moment before he spoke. "An' if ye find out,
ye'll go?"

"I have no other reason for staying."

He seemed indecisive, still, as if he did not trust me. "Ye'll
sell the haouse?" he wanted to know.

"I can't use it."

"I'll tell ye then," he said with abrupt decision. "Yer cousin,
him as was Abel Harrop, was took off by Them from Aoutside.
He called 'em an' They come." He paused as suddenly as he had
begun to speak, his dark eyes searching my face. "Ye dun't
believe," he cried. "Ye dun't know!"

"Know what?" I asked.

"Abaout Them from Aoutside." He looked distressed. "I

hadn't to a tol' ye, then. Ye'll pay no mind to me."

I tried to be patient, and explained once more that I wanted only to know what had happened to Abel.

But he was no longer interested in my cousin's fate. Still searching my face keenly, he demanded, "The books! Hev ye read the books?"

I shook my head.

"I tell ye to burn 'em—burn 'em all, afore it's too late!" He spoke with almost fanatic insistence. "I know whut's in 'em, summat."

It was this strange adjuration which ultimately sent me to the books my cousin had left.

That evening I sat down at the table where my cousin must so often have sat, by the light of the same lamp, with the chorus of whippoorwills already rising outside, to look with greater care at the book my cousin had been reading. I discovered almost at once, to my astonishment, that the print which I had mistaken for an old imitation of script was indeed script, and I had, further, the uncomfortable conviction that the manuscript, which had no title, was bound in human skin. Certainly it was very old, and it had the appearance of having been put together of scattered sheets of paper, on which its compiler had copied sentences and pages from books not his to own. Some of it was in Latin, some in French, some in English; though the writer's script was too execrable to permit any assurance in reading the Latin or French, I could make out the English after some study.

Most of it was plainly gibberish, but there were two pages which my cousin—or some previous reader—had marked in red crayon, and these I deemed must have been of some signal importance to Abel. I set about to make some sort of clarity out of the crabbed script. The first of them was fortunately short.

"To summon Yogge-Sothothe from the Outside, be wise to wait upon the Sun in the Fifth House, when Saturn is in trine; draw the pentagram of fire, and speak the Ninth Verse thrice, repeating which each Roodemas and Hallow's Eve causeth the Thing to breed in the Outside Spaces beyond the gate, of which Yogge-Sothothe is the Guardian. The once will not bring Him, but may bring Another Who is likewise desirous of growth, and if He have not the blood of Another, He may seek thine own. Therefore be not unwise in these things."

To this my cousin had written a postscript: "Cf. page 77 in *Text*."

Putting aside this reference, I turned to the other marked page, but no matter how carefully I read it, I could not make out of it anything but a highly fanciful rigmarole evidently copied faithfully from a far older manuscript—

"Concern'g yᵉ Old Ones, 'tis writ, they wait ev'r at yᵉ Gate, & yᵉ Gate is all places at all times, for They know noth'g of time or place but are in all time & in all place togeth'r without appear'g to be, & there are those amongst Them which can assume divers Shapes & Featurs & any gi'n Shape & any giv'n Face & yᵉ Gates are for Them ev'rywhere, but yᵉ 1st. was that which I caus'd to be op'd, Namely, in Irem, yᵉ City of Pillars, yᵉ City under yᵉ Desert, but wher'r men sayeth yᵉ forbidd'n Words, they shall cause there a Gate to be establish'd ·& shall wait upon Them Who Come through yᵉ Gate, ev'n as yᵉ Dhols, & yᵉ Abomin. Mi-Go, & yᵉ Tcho-Tcho peop., & yᵉ Deep Ones, & yᵉ Gugs, & yᵉ Gaunts of yᵉ Night & yᵉ Shoggoths & yᵉ Voormis, & yᵉ Shantaks which guard Kadath in yᵉ Colde Waste & yᵉ Plateau Leng. All are alike yᵉ Children of yᵉ Elder Gods, but yᵉ Great Race of Yith & yᵉ Gr. Old Ones fail'g to agree, one with another, & boath with yᵉ Elder Gods, separat'd, leav'g yᵉ Gr. Old Ones in possession of yᵉ Earth,

while ye Great Race, return'g from Yith took up Their Abode
forward in Time in Earth-Land not yet known to those who walk
ye Earth today, & there wait till there shall come again ye winds
& ye Voices which drove Them forth before & That which
Walketh on ye Winds over ye Earth & in ye spaces that are among
ye Stars forev'r."

I read this with amazement and wonder, but, since it meant
nothing to me, I returned to the original marked page and attempted to puzzle meaning out of that. I could not, save that I
had an uneasy memory of Amos Whateley's reference to "Them
Outside". I guessed, finally, that my cousin's appended note referred to the *R'lyeh Text;* so I took up this slender volume and
looked to the indicated page.

My language-study was unfortunately not thorough enough
to read the page with any sure meaning, but it appeared to be a
formula or chant summoning some ancient being in which
some primitive peoples had evidently once believed. I went
through it uncertainly in silence; then I read it slowly aloud, but
it seemed to have no greater meaning audibly, except only as a
curious aspect of ancient religious credos, for to such facets of
existence I deemed it was related.

By the time I rose wearily from the books, the whippoorwills
had once again taken possession of the valley. I put out the
light and looked into the moonlit darkness beyond the house.
The birds were there, as before; they made dark shadows on
the grass, on the roofs. In the moonlight they had a strange appearance of being uncannily distorted, and they were certainly
abnormally large birds. I had thought of whippoorwills as not
more than ten inches in length, but these birds were easily
twelve and fourteen inches long, and of an equivalent thick-

ness, so that they appeared singularly large. Doubtless, however, this was due to some trick of moonlight and shadow, act-
ing upon a tired and already overburdened imagination. But
there was no gainsaying the fact that the vehemence and loudness of their calls was in ratio to their apparently abnormal
size. There was considerably less movement among them that
night, however, and I had the uneasy conviction that they sat
there calling as if calling *to* someone or something or as if
waiting for something to happen, so that Hester Hutchins'
hushed urgent voice came back to mind with disturbing per-
sistence, "They're a-waitin' to ketch somebody's soul . . ."

II

The strange events which subsequently took place at my cousin's house date from that night. Whatever it was that set it in
motion, some malign force seemed to possess the entire valley.
Sometime during that night I woke, convinced that something
more than the ceaseless storming of the whippoorwills gave
voice in the moonlit dark. I lay listening, almost instantly wide
awake, listening for whatever it was, listening until the endless
whippoorwill screamed from a thousand throats seemed to
mark the very pulsing of my blood, the throbbing of the spheres!

Then I heard it—and listened—and doubted the evidence
of my own ears.

A kind of chanting, rising momentarily to ululation, but certainly in a tongue I did not know. Even now I cannot describe
it with any adequacy. Perhaps, if one could imagine turning on
several radio stations at once and listening to alien languages
pouring forth from each one, hopelessly jumbled, it might establish a sort of parallel. Yet, there seemed to be a kind of pat-

tern, and, try as I might, I could not disabuse myself of this notion. The gibberish I heard mingled uncannily with the crying of the whippoorwills. It reminded me of a litany, with the priest leading the recitative, and the audience murmuring in answer. The sound came intermittently, an odd predominance of consonants with but an occasional vowel. The most intelligible sounds, which seemed to be repeated, were these:

"Llllll-nglui, nnnnn-lagl, fhtagn-ngah, ai Yog-Sothoth!"

These were given voice in a crescendo of sound, bursting explosively at the last syllables, to which the whippoorwills responded in rhythmic song. It was not that they ceased crying, but only that when the other sounds came, the calling of the whippoorwills receded and faded as if into distance, then rushed forward and swelled out triumphantly in answer to the sounds in the night.

Strange and terrible as these sounds were, however, their source was even more frightening, for they came from somewhere within the house—either from the rooms above or from those below; and, with each moment that I listened, I became more and more convinced that the hideous gibberish I heard arose from somewhere within the room where I lay. It was as if the very walls pulsed with the sound, as if the entire house throbbed with this incredible mouthing, as if, indeed, my very being took part in this horror-fraught litany—not passively, but actively, even joyously!

How long I lay there virtually in a cataleptic state, I do not know. But eventually the invading sounds ceased; I was briefly aware of what seemed to be earth-shaking steps moving off into the heavens accompanied by a vast fluttering, as of whippoorwills rising from the roofs and the surrounding earth; then I fell into a deep sleep from which I did not awaken until mid-day.

I rose with alacrity then, for I meant to pursue my inquiry among my other neighbors with as much dispatch as possible. But I had intended, too, to look further into my cousin's books; yet that noon, when I came into the study and approached the table, I closed the book he had been reading and threw it carelessly to one side. I did this in full awareness of what I was doing, and yet with the intention of reading in it as much as I could. But there was something else lurking on the edge of my consciousness, a stubborn, unreasonable assurance that I knew all that was in this book, all that was in the rest of them piled here and there, and more than that, *much more.* And even as I took in this conviction, there seemed to rise up from deep inside me, as if it were from an ancestral memory to which I knew no bridge, a towering of awareness, and there crossed before my mind's eye vast and titanic heights and illimitable depths, and I saw great, amorphous beings like masses of protoplasmic jelly, thrusting forth tentacle-like appendages, standing on no known earth but on a dark, forbidding ground, devoid of vegetation, struck out gigantically against no known stars. And in the inner ear I heard names chanted and sung—*Cthulhu, Yog-Sothoth, Hastur, Nyarlathotep, Shub-Niggurath,* and many more—and I knew these for the Ancient Ones thrust forth by the Elder Gods and waiting now at the Gate to be summoned to their abode on earth as once in aeons past, and all the pomp and glory of serving them was clear to me, and I knew they would come again to wage their battle for the earth and all the peoples of the eartl and once more tempt the wrath of the Elder Gods, even as the poor, pitiable wretches of human kind tempted the wrath o their own fates! And I knew, as Abel knew, that their servants are the chosen ones who shall worship them and give them shelter, who shall house them and feed them until the time of their coming again, when the Gate is opened wide, and a thousand lesser Gates are opened to them in all the places of earth!

But this vision came and faded, like a flashing picture on a screen, from what source I could not tell. It was so brief, so momentary, that, when it had passed, the sound of the book's fall to the pile where I had thrown it still echoed in the room. I was shaken, for at one and the same time I knew my vision had no meaning and yet I knew it did have an importance out of all proportion to this house or this valley or even to all the world I knew.

I turned and went out of the house into the noon-day sun, and under its beneficent rays, the dark ordeal passed from me. I looked back to the house; it shone white in the sun, with the shadow of an elm lying upon it. I went then into the southeast, striking off through the long neglected fields and pastures toward the Whateley house, which lay about a mile away in that direction. Seth Whateley was a younger brother of Amos's; they had quarrelled years before, I had been told in Aylesbury, about what, no one knew, and now seldom saw or spoke to each other, despite living but two miles apart. Amos had grown close to the Dunwich Whateleys, who were, said the Aylesbury people, "the decayed branch" of one of the old armigerous families of Massachusetts.

The majority of the distance lay over the hill, through heavily wooded slopes and into the valley beyond, and quite often I started up whippoorwills, which flew on noiseless wings, circled a little, and settled horizontally on limbs or on the ground, blending wonderfully well with bark or old leaves, gazing at me with their small black eyes. Here and there, too, I saw eggs lying among the leaves. The hills were alive with whippoorwills, but I did not need this evidence to know that. It seemed to me a singular thing, however, that they should be ten times as numerous on the slope facing into Harrop's Valley than on those opposite. But they were. Descending the slope through the aromatic May woods to the valley where the Whateleys lived, I frightened up only one bird, which vanished noiselessly, and did not move away only a little and turn to regard me in passing. I did not think, then, that the curious attention of the whippoorwills on the near slope was frightening.

I was apprehensive about my reception at the Whateley house, and I soon found that I had good reason to be, for I was met by Seth Whateley carrying a gun, and giving me a stony stare from above that weapon.

"Ye got no call to bother us," he challenged as I approached.

Evidently he had just come from dinner, and had been on his way back to the fields when he caught sight of me; he had then retreated into the house and got his gun. Behind him I could see his wife, Emma, and their three children hanging on to her skirts, looking at me with fear plain in their eyes.

"I don't mean to bother you, Mr. Whateley," I said, as reassuringly as I could and with determined effort to suppress the irritation I felt at this unreasoning wall of suspicion which greeted me wherever I turned. "But I do mean to know what happened to my cousin Abel."

He gave me his stony stare briefly before replying, "We dun't know nuthin'. We ain't the kind to go pryin' araound. Whut yer cousin was a-doin' was his own business es long es he didn't bother us. Even if there's some things better let alone," he added darkly.

"Somebody must have made away with him, Mr. Whateley."

"He was took. That's whut they say my brother Amos says. He was took, body an' soul, an' if a man gits to lookin' where he hadn't oughta, that's whut's a-goin' to happen ev'ry time. No man's hand was raised agin him here—not but what there hadn't oughta hev bin."

"I'm going to find out. . . ."

He shifted his gun menacingly. "Ye can't do it here. I tol' you we dun't know nuthin'. An' we dun't. I ain't meanin' no offense, but the woman she's upset as all git-out, an' I dun't aim for her to be more turned out; so you git."

However crude Seth Whateley's invitation was, it was effective enough.

But matters were very much the same at Hough's, though there I was very poignantly aware of a greater tension in the atmosphere—not alone fear, but hatred, too. They were more civil, but anxious to be rid of me, and when at last I took my leave, with no word of help from them in my quest, I was convinced that, however they reasoned, the death of Laban Hough's wife was laid at my cousin's door. It was not evident in what was said so much as in what was not said; the charge lay in the unspoken words lurking behind their eyes and tongues. And I knew without needing to think further, but only by remembering how Hester Hutchins had talked to her cousin Flora about the whippoorwills calling for the souls of Benjy Wheeler and Sister Hough and Annie Begbie, that the whippoorwills and my cousin Abel Harrop were linked in the primitive superstition which haunted the waking and sleeping hours of these remote and earthy people; but by what bond these events could be connected, I could not guess. It was patent, moreover, that these people looked upon me with the same fear and dislike—or loathing—as they had looked upon Abel, and, whatever their reason for hating and fearing Abel had been, the same reason clearly applied to me in their limited capacity for thinking. Yet Abel, as I remembered him, had been even more sensitive than I, and, though surly by nature, he had always been essentially gentle, unwilling to hurt anyone, least of all a fellow-animal, human or otherwise. Doubtless their suspicions had taken rise in the well of dark superstition which is always rife in isolated countrysides, ever lurking ready to spark another Salem terror, and hound to death helpless victims innocent of any crime but knowledge.

It was that night, the night of the full moon, that the horror struck the Pocket.

But before I learned of what happened in the Pocket that night, I went through an ordeal of my own. It began soon after I got home from my last visit that afternoon, to the uncommunicative Osborns, across the hills to the north, after the sun had vanished beyond the western ridge, and I was at a meager supper. I began to have fancies again, and I couldn't get it out of my head that I wasn't alone in that house. So I left my supper and went through it, first downstairs, and then, taking the lamp —for the gable windows upstairs admitted little light—I went up. All the time I thought I could hear someone calling my name, someone calling to me in Abel's voice, the way it used to sound when we were children and played together here at this place, when his folks were living.

I found something in the store-room, something I could not

explain. I found it by accident because I saw that one of the panes was out of the window; I had not noticed that before. The room was filled with boxes and a little discarded furniture; it was stacked neatly enough, and in such a way that the most light could still filter into the room from the one window. Seeing the break, I went over to the window, and when I came around the boxes stacked there, I saw that there was a little space between the row of boxes and the window, enough for a chair and a man to sit in it. There was a chair there; there was no man, but there was some clothing that I knew for Abel's, and the way it lay there in the chair was enough to send a chill through me, though I don't know why I was so oddly frightened.

The fact was, the clothes lay there in the most peculiar manner. It was not as if somebody had laid them down like that; I don't think anyone *could* lay clothing just that way. I looked and looked at it, and I could not explain it in any other way but that somebody had been sitting there and just been pulled out of his clothes, as if he had been sucked out, and the clothes just collapsed with nothing inside them. I put the lamp down and touched them; they were not dusty to any extent; so that meant they had not been there long. I wondered if the sheriff's men had seen them, not that they could have made anything more out of them than I had; so I left them there, undisturbed, meaning to notify the sheriff next morning. But what with one thing and another, and everything that happened in the Pocket after that, I forgot about it; so the clothes are still there, sort of fallen together on the chair, just as I found them that night of the May full moon before the window in the store-room. And I set it down here and now, because it is evidence of what I claim, to stand against the terrible doubts that greet me on all sides.

That night the whippoorwills called with maddening insistence.

I heard them first while I was still in the store-room; they had begun to call out of the darkly wooded slopes from which the sunlight had gone, but far down the west, the sun had not set, and, though the Pocket was already in a kind of blue-hazed twilight, the sun still shone outside it, on the road connecting Arkham and Aylesbury. It was early for the whippoorwills, very early, earlier than they had ever called before. Irritated as I was already, by the stupid superstitious fear which had repelled every advance I made during the day, I know I could not stand yet another night of sleeplessness.

But soon the cries and calls were everywhere. *Whippoorwill! Whippoorwill! Whippoorwill!* Nothing but that monotonous screaming and screeching, the constant *Whippoorwill! Whippoorwill!* It pressed down from the hills into the valley, it crowded out of the moonlit night where the birds surrounded the house in a vast circle until it seemed that the house itself echoed their cries in a voice of its own, as if every joist and beam, every nail and stone, every board and shingle answered the thunder from outside, the horrible, the maddening *Whippoorwill! Whippoorwill! Whippoorwill!* rising in a cacophonous chorus which invaded and tore every fibre of my being. They made a wave of sound beating against the house, against the hills, once again as if they took part in some eldritch litany, and every cell in my body cried out in anguish at their noisome triumph.

It was about eight o'clock that evening when I knew I must do something. I had not brought any kind of weapon with me, and my cousin's shot-gun had been impounded by the sheriff and was still being held in the courthouse at Aylesbury; but I had found a stout cudgel under the couch where I slept—evidently my cousin's, to be kept at hand in case he was awakened suddenly in the night—and I meant to go out and kill as many of the whippoorwills as I could, in the hope that this would drive them away for good. I did not intend to go far; so I left the lamp burning in the study.

At my first step outside the door, the whippoorwills fluttered up, fanning out and away from me. But all my pent-up irritation and wrath burst forth; I ran in among them, swinging wildly, while they fluttered noiselessly up all about me, some of them silent now, but most of them still singing horribly. I pursued them out of the yard, up the road, into the woods, down across the road, back into the woods; I ran far, but how far I do not know, and I know that I killed many of them before I stumbled back to the house at last, exhausted, with only enough energy left to put out the lamp in the study, which had burned very low, and fall upon my couch. Before the distant whippoorwills which had escaped me could converge upon the house again, I was deep in slumber.

Because I do not know what time it was when I came in, I cannot say how long I slept before the ringing of the telephone woke me. Though the sun was already up, the hour was but five-thirty. As was now my habit, I went out into the kitchen, where the telephone was, and took down the receiver. That was how I learned about the coming of the horror.

"Mis' Wheeler, this's Emma Whateley. You heerd the news?"

"No, Mis' Whateley, ain't heerd a thing."

"Gawd! it's awful. It's Bert Giles. He's bin kilt. They found him jest abaout midnight thar whar the road goes acrost Giles' brook, near to the bridge. 'Twas Lute Corey found him, an' they say he let out a yell that woke Lem Giles up, an' the minute Lem heerd Lute hollerin', he knowed, he knowed all right. His ma begged Bert not to go to Arkham, but he was baound an' determined to go, you know haow set all them Gileses is. 'Pears he was a-goin' in with them Baxter men works Osborn's farm, summat under three mile from Gileses, an' he set out to walk to their place so's he could ride with 'em. Wa'n't no sign o' what kilt him, but Seth, who was daown come sunup this mornin' he says the graound's all tore up, like as if thar was a fight. An' he seen poor Bert, or what was left o' him. Gawd! Seth said his throat was all tore out an' his wrists tore open and his clothes jest about to shreds! An' that ain't all, even if 't is the worst. While Seth was a'standin' thar, Curtis Begbie he come runnin' up an' he said four o' Corey's cows they had night pasturin' in thet south forty was kilt, too, an' all tore up—jest like poor Bert!"

"Gawd!" whimpered Mrs. Wheeler, frightened. "Who will it be the next?"

"Sheriff says 'pears to be some wild animal, but thar hain't no tracks they could see. They bin workin' all araound ever since they got the word, an' Seth he says they hain't faound aout much."

"Oh, it's wuss'n when Abel was here."

"I allus said Abel wasn't the worst. I knowed. I knowed some of Seth's kin-folk—thet Wilbur an' Ol' Whateley—an' they're a sight worse'n a feller like Abel Harrop was. I knowed it, Mis' Wheeler. An' thar's others at Dunwich, too—the Whateleys ain't the only ones."

"If it ain't Abel. . . ."

"An' Seth, he says durin' that time he was a-standin' thar lookin' at poor Bert Giles, Amos come up, Amos that ain't said ten words to Seth in ten years, an' he jest took one look an' he kind o' muttered to hisself an' Seth says he said, 'That dam' fool spoke the words!' jest like that, an' Seth, he turns to him an' he says, 'Whut's thet you're sayin', Amos?' An' Amos he looks at him an' he says, 'Ain't nothin' es bad es a fool whut don't know whut he's got!' "

"Thet Amos Whateley allus was a bad one, Mis' Whateley, an' that's a fact, an' it don't make no difference you're related, it's jest the same."

"Ain't nobody knows it better'n I do, Mis' Wheeler."

By this time other women had joined the conversation, identifying themselves. Mrs. Osborn came on the wire to say that the Baxters, tiring of waiting, and thinking that Bert had changed his mind, had gone on to Arkham. They had come back about eleven-thirty. Hester Hutchins predicted that this was "only the beginnin'. Amos said it." Vinnie Hough cried hysterically that she was of a mind to take the children, her niece and nephew, and flee to Boston until the devil "took his stand somewhere's else." It was only when Hester Hutchins began to tell the rest of them, wildly, that Jesse Trumbull had come in and reported that all the blood had been sucked out of Bert Giles' body and also out of the four Corey cows that I hung up; I could recognize the beginning of the legend and the working of superstition beginning to be constructed on the few pertinent facts.

Throughout the day there were various reports. At noon the sheriff stopped in perfunctorily to inquire whether I had heard anything in the night, but I replied that I was incapable of hearing anything but whippoorwills. Since everyone else to whom he had talked mentioned having heard the whippoorwills, he was not surprised. He volunteered the information that Jethro Corey had awakened in the night and had heard the cows bellowing, but before he could get dressed to go down they had stopped; so he had assumed they had been disturbed by some animal passing through the pasture—the hills abounded in fox and raccoon—and had gone back to bed. Mamie Whateley had heard someone scream; she was sure that it was Bert, but, since she reported it only after having heard all the details of the killing, it was thought that this was only an imaginative afterthought, a pathetic attempt to focus a little attention on herself. After the sheriff had gone, one of his deputies stopped in, too, plainly worried, because their failure to solve the mystery of my cousin's disappearance was already a blot on their record, and this new crime might well bring them further criticism. Apart from these visits and the steady ringing of the telephone, I was not disturbed throughout the day, and I managed to get a little sleep in anticipation of the night's infesting whippoorwills.

Yet that night, curiously, the whippoorwills, for all their damnable calling, did me a good turn. I had gone to sleep, surprisingly, despite their cacophonous cries, and had slept perhaps two hours, when I was awakened. I thought at first that dawn had come, but it had not, and then I realized that what had awakened me was the absence of the whippoorwills' voices; their sudden cessation and the succeeding silence had startled me from my sleep. This curious and unprecedented occurrence fully aroused me; I got up, pulled on my trousers, and went to the window to look out.

I saw a man running from the yard—a big man. I thought at once of what had happened to Albert Giles the night before, and a momentary fear took possession of me, for a big man could perhaps have wreaked the night's havoc, a big man and a homicidal maniac—but then I knew that there was only one man so big in all the valley, and that was Amos Whateley. And the direction in which he was vanishing in the moonlight was that of the Hutchins place, where he worked. My impulse to set out after him, to shout at him, was halted by what I then saw out of the corner of my eyes—a sudden, fitful orange glow. I threw up the window and craned out. Down along one corner the house was burning!

Because I acted without delay, and because a bucket of water already stood under the pump, I was able to put the fire out without the burning of more than a square foot or two of siding and some further charring. But it was clear that the fire had been set, and undoubtedly by Amos Whateley, and, had it not been for the whippoorwills' strange silence, I might have perished in the holocaust. As it was, I was badly shaken, for if my neighbors bore me such ill-feeling as to take such measures to drive me from my cousin's house, what might I still expect of them? Yet, opposition has always strengthened me; and after a few moments, it was again true. I felt convinced anew that it was my search for the facts behind my cousin's disappearance alarmed them to such a degree as this, then I was on the right track in believing that they knew far more about it than any of them was willing to tell. So I went back to bed determined to face Amos Whateley next day, when I could find him somewhere in the fields, away from the Hutchins house, and we could talk without being overheard.

Accordingly, in mid-morning I sought out Amos Whateley. He was at work in the same hilltop field where he had worked when first I saw him, but this time he did not come to confront me; instead, he stopped the horses and stood watching me. I saw, as I came up toward the stone fence there that his bearded face held both apprehension and defiance. He stood unmoving, save that he pushed his crumpled felt hat farther back on his head; his lips were pressed together in a firm, unyielding line, but his eyes were wary. Since he was not far from the fence, I stopped where I was, along the woods' edge.

"Whateley, I saw you set fire to my house last night," I said. "Why?"

There was no answer.

"Come, come—I came up here to talk to you. I could just as easily go into Aylesbury and talk to the sheriff."

"Ye read the books," he spat forth hoarsely. "I tol' ye not tew. Ye read thet place aout laoud; I know ye did. Ye opened the Gate, an' Them from Aoutside kin come. Wa'n't like yer cousin—he called 'em an' They come—but he didn't do whut They wanted; so They took him. But he didn't know, ye didn't larn how tew, an' They're a-settin' right this minute in this valley an' nobody knows whut'll happen next."

It took me a few minutes to make sense out of this rigmarole, and even then it was only a sort of sense, not logical, by any means. Amos apparently meant to suggest that by reading aloud a passage from the book my cousin had been reading, I had invited some force or being from "outside" into the valley— doubtless an integral part of the natives' absurd superstitions.

"I haven't seen any strangers about," I said curtly.

"Ye dun't allus *see* 'em. Cousin Wilbur says They kin take any shape They like an' They kin git inside ye an' They kin eat through yer mouth an' see through yer eyes, an' if ye hain't got the pertection, They kin take ye the way They took yer cousin. Ye dun't see 'em," he went on, his voice rising now to almost a scream, "because they're inside ye this minute."

I waited for his hysteria to diminish a little. "And what do They eat?" I asked quietly.

"Ye know!" he cried vehemently. "Blood an' sperit—blood to make 'em grow, sperit to make 'em wise to human-kind. Laugh, if ye wants tew, but ye ought tew know. They 'hippoor'lls knows, all right—thet's why they're allus a-singin' an' a-callin' daown by yer place."

I could not help smiling, though his earnestness was not to be questioned and forestalled the laughter he had thought was coming.

"But that doesn't explain why you should try to burn my house down—and me, too, for all I know."

"I didn't mean ye no harm, but I wanted for ye to git. If ye hain't got no house, ye can't stay."

"And do you represent the opinion of all the others?"

"I know the most," he said, with a faint pride showing through his defiant apprehension. "My Granpaw hed the books, an' he tol' me lots, an' Cousin Wilbur, he knowed, too, an' I know thar's lots o' things the rest dun't know abaout whut goes on aout thar—" he waved one arm toward the heavens—"or daown thar"—he pointed underfoot—"an' lots they needn't to know, less'n it'd scare 'em. An' only half-knowin' it's wuss'n nuthin' a-tall. Ye should-a burnt them books, Mr. Harrop—I tol' ye. It's too late naow."

I searched his face in vain for any sign to show that he was not serious; he was wholly sincere, even a little regretful, as if he were sorry he had to consign me to whatever nameless fate he foresaw. For a moment I was uncertain as to how to deal with him. One cannot simply overlook an attempt to burn one's house down, and, for all I knew, one's self with it.

"Very well, Amos. Whatever it is you know is your affair. But I know you set fire to my house, and I can't overlook that. I'll expect you to make that right. When you have the time, you can come down and repair it; if you do that, I'll not report you to the sheriff."

"Nuthin' else either?"

"What else?"

"If ye dun't know. . . ." He shrugged. "I'll come soon's I'm able."

However ridiculous his rigmarole had been, what he said did disconcert me, largely because there was a wild kind of logic to it. But then, I reflected, as I walked back through the woods to my cousin's house, there is a perverted kind of logic to all superstition, which explains the tenacity of superstitions from one generation to another. Yet there had also been unmistakable fear in Amos Whateley, a fear unaccountable except by superstition, for Whateley was a powerful man who could in all probability have tossed me over the stone fence that separated us, with a heave of one arm. And in Whateley's attitude lay the undeniable germ of something profoundly disturbing, if only I could have access to the key.

III

I come now to that portion of my account which must remain unfortunately obscure, for I cannot always be sure of the precise order or meaning of the events in which I took part. Disturbed as I was by Whateley's rigmarole of superstitious fear, I went directly back to my cousin's house and turned to the strange old books which constituted his library. I sought some further clue to Whateley's curious beliefs, and yet, I had no sooner picked up one of the books than I was once again filled with the un-shakable conviction that this search was futile, for what does it gain a man to read that which he already knows? And what they think who know nothing of these things—what do they matter? For it seemed as if I saw again that strange landscape with its titanic amorphous beings, and it was as if I heard again the chanting of alien names, hinting of terrible power, a chanting accompanied by a fluting of music, and a choral ululation from throats which were not human.

This illusion lasted but momentarily, only long enough to deflect me from my purpose. I abandoned any further examina-tion of my cousin's book, and after a light lunch I made another attempt to pursue my inquiry into my cousin's disappearance, with such lack of success that I gave it up in mid-afternoon and returned to the house in an indecisive frame of mind, no longer so certain that the men from the sheriff's office had not done all in their power to trace Abel. And, though my resolve was not diminished, I began for the first time to have grave doubts of my ability to carry on.

That night I heard strange voices once again.

Or perhaps I should not say "strange", for I had heard them before; they were unidentifiable and alien, and once again their source was a mystery to me. But that night the whippoorwills were louder than ever before; their cries rang piercingly in the house and in the Pocket outside. The voices began, I should judge, at about nine o'clock. It was a cloudy night, with great grey banks pressing close upon the hills and the valley, and the air was moist; its very moisture, however, increased the loudness of the whippoorwills and intensified the strange voices which welled forth suddenly, without preamble, as once before —outré, unintelligible, eldritch—they were all that and more, defying description. And once again there was the effect as of a litany, with the chorus of whippoorwills swelling forth as if in answer to every chanted sentence or phrase, an unbearable cacophony of noise that rose to frightful cataclysms of sound.

For a while I strove to make something out of the alien voices which throbbed in the room, but they were not coherent, they had the sound of gibberish, despite my inmost conviction that, far from gibberish, they were significant and ominous, beautiful and terrible, suggestive and fraught with meaning far beyond my ability to grasp. Nor did I any longer much care from whence they came; I knew that they rose from somewhere within the house, but whether by virtue of some natural phenomenon or by other agency, I could not determine. They were the product of darkness, or—and I could not gainsay the possibility—they might well have arisen in a consciousness deeply disturbed by the demoniac crying of the whippoorwills, making their terrible bedlam on all sides, filling valley and house and mind with nothing but their thunder, piercing and rasping, the constant, shrilling *Whippoorwill! Whippoorwill! Whippoorwill!*

I lay in a state akin to catalepsy, listening:

"Lllllll-nglui, nnnn-lagl, fhtagn-nagh, ai Yog-Sothoth!"

The whippoorwills answered in a rolling crescendo of sound that flowed upon the house, broke against it, invaded it; and in the recession of voices, the echo came back from the hills, crashing upon my consciousness with only slightly diminished force.

"*Y gnaiih! Y'bthnk. EEE-ya-ya-ya-yahaaahaahaahaaa!*"

And again the explosion of sound, the incessant *Whippoorwill! Whippoorwill! Whippoorwill!* beating upon the night and the cloudy darkness like the throbbing of thousands upon thousands of wild drums!

Mercifully, I lost consciousness.

The human body and mind can tolerate only so much before oblivion comes, and with oblivion that night came a dream-structure of unutterable power and terror. I dreamed I was in a far place, a place of vast monolithic buildings, inhabited not by men, but by beings apart from the wildest imagination of men, a land of great unknown tree ferns, of Calamites and Sigillaria surrounding the fantastic buildings of that place, of fearsome forests of trees and other growths belonging to no known terrestrial place. Here and there rose colossi of black stone, deep in places where perpetual twilight held sway, and in some areas there were basaltic ruins of incredible age. And in such night-held places, the constellations which shone forth resembled no known map of the heavens I had ever seen, nor did the topography of the land in those places bear any resemblances to anything I had known, save only certain artists' conceptions of earth in prehistoric times dating far beyond the Paleozoic period.

Of the beings who inhabited the dream I remember only that they were of no fixed shape, gigantic in size, and possessed of appendages which were in the nature of tentacles, but afforded locomotion as well as the power to grasp and hold objects; and these appendages were capable of being retracted in one place and of coming forth in another. They were the inhabitants of the monolithic buildings, and many of them were inert in sleep, at which they were attended by foetal beings considerably smaller in size, but of related structure in that they too were capable of changing shape. They were of a horrible, fungoid color, not flesh-colored at all; in this they resembled the color of many of the buildings, and at times they appeared to alter horribly in shape, as if in caricature of the curvilinear types of masonry so prevalent in various parts of that dream-world.

Strangely, the chanting and the crying of the whippoorwills continued as an integral part of the dream, but in perspective, rising and falling in the background, as in the distance. And it seemed, moreover, as if I, too, existed in that strange place, but on a different plane, as if I, too, served one of the Great Ones there, going forth into the fearsome darkness of the alien forests to slaughter beasts and open their veins so that the Great Ones might feed and grow in other dimensions but that of their weird world.

How long the dream lasted, I could not say. I slept all night, and yet was tired out of all proportion when I woke, as if I had worked most of the night and got but little sleep. I dragged myself wearily to the kitchen and fried myself some bacon and eggs, after which I sat listlessly to eat them. However, breakfast with several cups of black coffee gave me new life, and I rose from the table feeling refreshed.

While I was outside for wood, the telephone rang. It was Hough's ring, but I hurried in to listen.

I recognized Hester Hutchins' voice at once, having become accustomed to her ever-wagging tongue. "An' they do say es thar was six, seven kilt. The bes' caows in his herd, Mr. Osborn said. They was up in thet south forty—thet's his nearest pasture

to Harrop's Pocket. Gawd knows haow many others would o'
bin kilt if twa'n't fer the rest o' the herd bustin' down the fence
an' gittin' daown to the barn. Thet's haow come Osborn's hired
man, Andy Baxter, went up to the pasture with a lantern an'
seen 'em. Jest like them Corey caows, an' poor Bert Giles—
throats all tore aout, an' them poor beasts beat up suthin' turrible! Gawd knows whut's loose in the Pocket, Vinnie, but
suthin's got to be done or we'll all be kilt. I knowed them whippoorwills was a-callin' for somebody's soul, an' they got poor
Bert's. They're still a-callin' an' I know whut thet means, an'
you do, too, Vinnie Hough—they's to be more souls a-comin' to
them whippoorwills afore the moon changes onct more."

"Gawd-a-mercy! I'm goin' straight to Boston, soon's I kin git
away."

I knew the sheriff would stop in again that day, and I was
ready for him when he came. I had heard nothing. I explained
that I had been exhausted the night before but had managed to
sleep in spite of the din made by the whippoorwills. In turn,
he very considerately told me what had been done to Osborn's
cows. Seven of them had been slaughtered, he said, and there
was something very strange about it, for no cow had bled very
much, despite the way in which each throat was ripped. And,
in spite of the bestial manner of the attack, it seemed plain that
it had been done by a man, for there were fragmentary footprints in evidence, unfortunately not complete enough to warrant attempting to make any kind of observation. However, he
went on in confidence, one of his men had had his eye on Amos
Whateley for some time; Amos had been making very queer
remarks, and his actions had been those of a man who expected
that he was being followed or something. The sheriff said this

wearily, for he was tired, having been up since he had been called to Osborn's farm. And what did I know about Whateley? he went on.

I shook my head and confessed that I knew all too little about any of my neighbors. "But I've noticed his queer talk," I admitted. "Whenever I've talked with him, he's said very strange things."

The sheriff leaned forward eagerly. "Did he ever talk or mutter about 'feeding' someone something?"

I admitted that Amos had so talked.

The sheriff seemed satisfied. He took his leave after indirectly scoring me for my own conspicuous lack of success in discovering what had happened to my cousin Abel. I was not unduly surprised at his suspicions of Amos Whateley. And yet there was something in sharp conflict with the sheriff's theory deep in my own awareness, and a kind of uneasiness burgeoned there, like the nagging memory of something left undone.

My exhaustion did not leave me during the day, and I did little work, though I found it necessary to wash some of my clothing which had somehow become rust-stained. I took time, too, to examine my cousin's work on the fish-netting, and it occurred to me that he had designed it to catch something. And what more likely than that it was the whippoorwills, which must have driven him, too, to his wits' end now and then? Or perhaps he knew more of their habits than I did, and perhaps he had a better reason to try to catch them than their constant crying.

I slept when I could during that day, though from time to time I listened to the current of frightened talk that went on over the telephone. There was no end to it; the telephone rang all day long, and sometimes the men talked to each other, as well as the women, who had heretofore monopolized the wires. They talked about pooling herds of cows and setting a watch on them, but then, fearful, none wanted to watch alone; they spoke of keeping their cows in the barns at night, and I gathered that they had decided to do this. The women, however, wanted no one to go out after dark for any reason whatsoever.

"It dun't come by day," Emma Whateley insisted to Marie Osborn. "Ain't never bin nuthin' done by day. So I say a body should stay close to hum onct the sun gits down over the hills."

And Lavinia Hough had taken off for Boston, just as she said she would, with the children.

"Up an' took them kids an' let Laban be thar," said Hester Hutchins. "But he ain't alone; he's fetched a man out from Arkham to set with him. Oh, it's a turrible thing, it's a Gawd's punishment on us, an' the wusst is nobody knows whut It looks like nor whar It comes from 'r nuthin'."

An the superstition about the cows being drained of blood was repeated again.

"They said them caows didn't bleed much, an' that's why—they didn't hev no blood left to bleed," said Angeline Wheeler. "Gawd, whut's a-goin' to happen to us all? We can't jest set here an' wait till we're all kilt."

This frightened conversation was a sort of whistling in the dark; the telephones gave them, men as well as women, a sense of being less isolated, less solitary. That none of them ever called me I did not ponder; I was an outsider, and people from outside are seldom taken into country circles like that of my neighbors around Harrop's Pocket in short of ten years' time—

if then. Toward evening I no longer listened on the telephone, being still very tired.

On the next night but one the voices came again.

And the dream came, too. Once more I was in a vast place of strange basalt buildings and fearsome forest growths. And I knew that in that place I was a Chosen One, proud to serve the Ancient Ones, belonging to that greatest of all, who was like the others and yet unlike them, that one among them who alone could take the form of a congeries of shining globes, the Guardian of the Threshold, the Keeper of the Gate, Great Yog-Sothoth, biding his time to return to his one-time terrestrial plane, where I must continue to serve him. Oh, the power and the glory! Oh, the wonder and the terror! Oh, the eternal bliss! And I heard the whippoorwills crying, their voices rising and falling in the background of that place, while the chanters cried out under the alien stars, under the alien heaven, into the gulfs and to the shrouded peaks, cried out aloud—

"Lllllll-nglui, nnnn-lagl, fhtagn-ngah, ai Yog-Sothoth!"

And I, too, raised my voice in praise of Him, the Lurker at the Threshold . . .

"Lllllll-nglui, nnnn-lagl, fhtagn-ngah, ai Yog-Sothoth!"

That is what they say I was screaming when they found me crouching beside the body of poor Amelia Hutchins, tearing at her throat—the helpless woman struck down on her way back along the ridge path from a visit to Abbey Giles. That is what they say I mouthed in my bestial rage, with the whippoorwills all around, crying and screaming in their maddening voices. And that is why they have locked me into this room with the bars at the window. Oh, the fools! The fools! Having failed once with Abel, they grasp at straws. How can they think to keep one of the Chosen Ones from Them? What are bars to Them?

But they are trying to frighten me when they say I have done these things. I never raised my hand against any human being. I have told them how it was, if only they would see. I told them. It was not I, never! No, I know who it was. I think I have always known, and if they look, they will find proof.

It was the whippoorwills, the incessantly calling whippoorwills, the damnable, lurking whippoorwills waiting out there, the whippoorwills, the whippoorwills in the hills . . .

Something in Wood

IT IS FORTUNATE that the limitations of the human mind do not often permit viewing in proper perspective all the facts and events upon which it touches. I have thought this many times particularly in regard to the curious circumstances surrounding the disappearance of Jason Wecter, music and art critic of the Boston *Dial*, which took place a year ago and about which many theories were advanced, ranging from a suspicion of murder by some disappointed artist, smarting under Wecter's biting invective, to the belief that Wecter simply took off for parts unknown, without word to anyone, and for a reason known only to himself.

This latter belief comes closer to actuality, perhaps, than is commonly supposed, though its acceptance is a matter of terminology, and involves the question of whether or not Wecter's absence was voluntary or involuntary. There is, however, one explanation which offers itself to those who are imaginative enough to grasp it, and the certain circumstances surrounding the event lead, indeed, to no other conclusion. In these circumstances I had a part, not a small one, by any means, though it was not recognized as such even by me until after the fact of Jason Wecter's vanishing.

These events began with the expression of a wish, than which nothing could be more prosaic. Wecter, who lived alone in an old house in King's Lane, Cambridge, well away from the beaten thoroughfare, was a collector of primitive art work, preferably in wood or stone; he had such things as the strange religious carvings of the Penitentes, the bas-reliefs of the Mayas, the outré sculptures of Clark Ashton Smith, the wooden fetish figures and the carvings of gods and goddesses out of the South Sea islands, and many others; and he had wished for something in wood that might be "different", though the pieces by Smith seemed to me to offer as much variety as anyone could wish. But Smith's were not in wood; Wecter wanted something in wood to balance his collection, and, admittedly, he had nothing in wood save some few masks from Ponape which came close to the strange and wonderful imagery of the Smith sculptures.

I suppose that more than one of his friends was looking for something in wood for Jason Wecter, but it fell to my lot to find it one day in an out-of-the-way second-hand shop in Portland, where I had gone for a holiday—a strange piece indeed, but exquisitely done, a kind of bas-relief of an octopoid creature rising out of a broken, monolithic structure in a sub-aqueous setting. The price of four dollars was extremely reasonable, and the fact that I could not interpret the carving was, if anything, all the more likely to add to its value in Wecter's eyes.

I have described the "creature" as "octopoid", but it was not an octopus. What it was I did not know; its appearance suggested a body much longer than and different from that of an octopus, and its tentacular appendages issued not only from its face, as if from the place where a nose ought to be—much as in the Smith sculpture, *Elder God*—but also from its sides and from the central part of its body. The two appendages issuing from its face were clearly prehensile and were carved in an attitude of flaring outward, as if about to grasp, or grasping, something. Immediately above these two tentacles were deep-set eyes, carved with uncanny skill, so that the impression was one of vast and disturbing evil. At its base there was carved a line in no known language:

Ph'nglui mglw'nafh Cthulhu R'lyeh wgah'nagl fhtagn.

Of the nature of the wood in which it was carved—a dark brown, almost black wood with a hitherto unfamiliar grain of many whorls—I knew nothing, save that it was unusually heavy for wood. Though it was larger than I had in mind to get for Jason Wecter, I knew that he would like it.

Where had it come from? I asked the phlegmatic little man behind the cluttered desk. He raised his spectacles to his forehead and said that he could tell me no more than that it had come out of the Atlantic. "Maybe washed off some vessel," he hazarded. It had been brought in with other things but a week or two ago by an old fellow who habitually scavenged along the coast for such pieces among the debris washed up by the sea. I asked what it might represent, but of this the proprietor knew even less than of its source. Jason was therefore free to invent any legend he chose to account for it.

He was delighted with the piece, and especially because he discovered immediately certain startling similarities between it and the stone sculptures by Smith. As an authority on primitive art, he pointed out another factor which made it clear that the proprietor of the shop from which I had obtained it had practically given it to me at four dollars—certain marks which indicated that the piece had been made by tools far older than those of our own time, or indeed, of the civilized world as we knew it.

These details were but of passing interest to me, of course, since I did not share Wecter's liking for primitives, but I confess to feeling an unaccountable revulsion at Wecter's juxtaposition of this octopoid carving with Smith's work, arising out of unvoiced questions which troubled me—if indeed this thing were centuries old, as Wecter inferred, and represented no known kind of carving previously recognized, how came it that the modern sculptures of Clark Ashton Smith bore such resemblance to it?—and was it not more than a coincidence that Smith's figures created out of the stuff of his weird fiction and poetry, should parallel the art of someone removed many hundreds of years in time and leagues in space from him?

But these questions were not asked. Perhaps if they had been, subsequent events might have been altered. Wecter's enthusiasm and delight were accepted as tributes to my judgment and the carving placed on his wide mantel with the best of his wooden pieces; there I was content to leave it, and to forget it.

It was a fortnight before I saw Jason Wecter again, and I would perhaps not have seen him immediately on my return to Boston if it had not been for my attention being called to a particularly savage criticism of a public showing of the sculptures of Oscar Bogdoga, whose work Wecter had given high praise only two months before. Indeed, Wecter's review of his show was of such a nature as to excite the disturbed interest of many mutual friends; it indicated a new approach to sculpture on Wecter's part, and promised many surprises to those who regularly followed his criticisms. However, one of our mutual acquaintances who was a psychiatrist, confessed to some alarm over the curious allusions manifest in Wecter's short but remarkable article.

I read it with mounting surprise, and immediately observed certain distinct departures from Wecter's customary manner. His charge that Bogdoga's work lacked "fire . . . the element of suspense . . . any pretense of spirituality" was usual enough; but the assertions that the artist "evidently had no familiarity with the cult-art of Ahapi or Ahmnoida" and that Bogdoga might have done better than a hybrid imitation of "the Ponape school" were not only inapropos but completely out of character, for Bogdoga was a mid-European whose heavy masses bore far more similarity to those of Epstein than to the work of, for instance, Mestrovic, and certainly none at all to the primitives which were such a delight to Wecter, and which had manifestly now begun to affect his judgment. For Wecter's entire article was studded with strange references to artists no one had even heard of, to places far in space and time, if indeed they were of this earth, and to culture patterns which bore no relation whatever to any at all familiar even to informed readers.

Yet his approach to Bogdoga's art had not been entirely unanticipated, for he had only two days before written a critique of a new symphony by Franz Hoebel given its initial performance by the flamboyant and egocentric Fradelitski, filled with references to "the fluted music of the spheres," and "those piped notes, pre-Druidic in origin, which haunted the aether long before mankind raised an instrument of any kind to hands or lips." At the same time he had hailed a playing, on the same program, of Harris's *Symphony Number 3*, which he had publicly detested previously, as "a brilliant example of a return to that preprimitive music which haunts the ancestral consciousness of mankind, the music of the Great Old Ones, emerging despite the overlayer of Fradelitski—but then, Fradelitski, having no creative music in him, must of necessity impose upon every work under his baton enough Fradelitski to gratify his ego, no matter how much it may slander the composer."

These two utterly mystifying reviews sent me in haste to Wecter's home, where I found him brooding at his desk with the offending reviews and a sizable stack of letters—doubtless in protest—before him.

"Ah, Pinckney," he greeted me, "no doubt you too are brought here by these curious reviews of mine."

"Not exactly," I hedged. "Recognizing that any criticism stems from personal opinions, you're at liberty to write what you like, as long as you're sincere. But who the devil are Ahapi and Ahmnoida?"

"I wish I knew."

He spoke so earnestly that I could not doubt his sincerity.

"But I haven't a doubt that they existed," he went on. "Just as the Great Old Ones appear to have some status in ancient lore."

"How did you come to refer to them if you don't know who they are?" I asked.

"I can't entirely explain that, either, Pinckney," he answered, a troubled frown on his face. "But I can try."

Thereupon he launched into a not entirely coherent account of certain things which had happened to him ever since his acquisition of the octopoidal carving I had found in Portland. He had not spent a night free of dreams in which the strange creature of the carving existed, either in the foreground or ever aware on the rim of his dream. He had dreamed of subterrene places and of cities beneath the sea; he had seen himself in the

Carolines and in Peru; he had walked by dream under leering gambrel-roofed houses, in legend-haunted Arkham; he had ridden in strange sea-going craft to places beyond the reaches of the known oceans. The carving, he knew, was a miniature, for the creature was a great, protoplasmic being, capable of changing shape in myriad ways. Its name, said Pinckney, was *Cthulhu;* its domain was *R'lyeh,* an awesome city far under the Atlantic. It was one of the Great Old Ones, who were believed to be reaching from other dimensions and far stars, as well as from the sea's depths and pockets in space for re-establishment of their ancient dominion over earth. It appeared accompanied by amorphous dwarfs, clearly sub-human, which went before it playing strange pipes making music of no known parallel. Apparently the carving, which had been made in very ancient times, very probably before any kind of human record was kept, but after the dawn of mankind, by artisans in the Carolines, was a "point of contact" from the alien dimension inhabited by the beings which sought return.

I confess that I listened with some misgivings, noticing which, Wecter stopped talking abruptly, rose, and brought the octopoidal carving from the mantel to his desk. He put it down before me.

"Look at that carefully, now, Pinckney. Do you see anything different about it?"

I examined it with care, and announced finally that I could see no alteration.

"It doesn't seem to you that the extended tentacles from the face are—let us put it 'more extended'?"

I said it did not. But even as I spoke I could not be certain. The suggestion is all too often father of the fact. Was there an extension or not? I could not say then; I cannot say now. But plainly Wecter believed that some extension had taken place. I examined the carving anew, and felt again that curious revulsion I had first experienced at noticing the similarity between the sculptures of Smith and this curious piece.

"It doesn't strike you, then, that the ends of the tentacles have lifted and pushed out further?" he pressed.

"I can't say it does."

"Very well." He took the carving and restored it to its place on the mantel.

Coming back to his desk, he said, "I'm afraid you'll think me deranged, Pinckney, but the fact is that ever since I've had this in my study, I've been aware of existing in what I can only describe as dimensions different from those we commonly know, dimensions, in short, such as those I've dreamed about. For instance, I have no memory of having written these reviews; yet they are mine. I find them in my script, in my proofs, in my column. I know, in short, that I and no one else wrote these reviews. I cannot publicly disown them, though I realize very well that they contradict opinions set down over my signature many times before this. Yet it cannot be denied that there is a curiously impressive logic running through them; since reading them—and, incidentally, the indignant letters I have received about them—I have given the matter some study. Contrary to the opinions you may have heard me express previously, the work of Bogdoga *does* have a relationship to a hybrid form of early Carolinian cult-art, and the third *Symphony* of Harris *does* have a marked and disturbing appeal to the primitive, so that one must ask whether their initial offensiveness to traditionally sensitive or cultured people is not an instinctive reaction against the primitive which the inner self instantly acknowledges."

He shrugged. "But that's neither here nor there, is it, Pinck-ney? The fact is that the carving you found in Portland has exercised an irrationally disturbing influence on me to such an extent that I am sometimes not sure whether it has been for the best or not."

"What kind of influence, Jason?"

He smiled strangely. "Let me tell you how I feel it. The first night I was aware of it was that immediately after you left it here. There was a party here that evening, but by midnight the guests were gone, and I was at my typewriter. Now then, I had a prosaic piece to do—something about a little piano recital by one of Fradelitski's pupils, and I got it off in no time at all. But all the time I was aware of that carving. Now, I was aware of it on two planes; the one was that on which it came into my possession, as a gift from you, an object of no great size, and clearly three-dimensional; the other was an extension—or invasion, if you like—into a different dimension, in relation to which I existed in this room against the carving as a seed to a pumpkin. In short, when I had finished the brief notice I wrote I had only the odd illusion that the carving had grown to unimaginable proportions; for a cataclysmic instant I felt that it had added concrete being, that it was reared up before me as a colossus against which I stood as a pathetic miniature. This lasted but a moment; then it withdrew. Note that I say it withdrew; it did not just cease to exist; no, it seemed to compress, to draw back, precisely as if it were drawing out of this new dimension to return to its actual state as it must exist before my eyes—but as it need not exist before my psychic perception. This has continued; I assure you, it is not an hallucination, though I see by your expression that you are thinking I've taken leave of my senses."

It was not as bad as that, I hastened to assure him. What he said was either true or it was not; the presumptive evidence, based on the concrete facts of his strange reviews, indicated that he was sincere; therefore, for Jason Wecter, what he said was true. It must therefore have meaning and motivation.

"Postulating that everything you say is true," I said at last, cautiously, "there must be some reason for it. Perhaps you're working too hard, and this is an extension of your own sub-conscious."

"Good old Pinckney!" he exclaimed, laughing.

"Or, if it is not, it must then have some motivation—from outside."

His smile vanished; his eyes narrowed. "You concede that, do you, Pinckney?"

"Presumptively, yes."

"Good. So I thought after my third experience. Twice I was perfectly willing to lay to sensory illusion; three times, no. The hallucinations experienced as a result of eye-strain are seldom as elaborate as that, tend to be limited to imaginary rats, dots, and the like. So then, if this creature belongs to a cult in that it is the object of worship—and I understand that its worship extends into our own day, though secretly—there seems to be but one explanation. I return to what I said before—that carving is a focal point of contact from another dimension in time or space; granting that, then plainly the creature is at-tempting to reach through to me."

"How?" I asked bluntly.

"Ah, I am not a mathematician, not a scientist. I am only a music and art critic. That conclusion represents the outside limits of my extra-cultural knowledge."

The hallucination had appeared to persist. Moreover, it had had an existence in his sleeping hours on yet another plane in that, during sleep, Wecter accompanied the creature of the carving without difficulty into other dimensions outside our own space and time. Consistent illusions are not rarities in medical case-histories, nor are those which develop progressively, but such an experience as Jason Wecter's was clearly more than illusory, since it extended insidiously into his very thought-patterns. I mused on this for a long time that night, turning over and over in my mind everything he had told me about the Elder Gods, the Great Old Ones, the mythological entities and their worshippers, into the culture pattern of which Wecter's interest had penetrated with such disturbing results for him.

Thereafter I watched the *Dial* apprehensively for Jason Wecter's column.

Because of what he wrote in the intervening ten days before I saw him again, Jason Wecter was soon the talk of cultural Boston and the surrounding countryside. Surprisingly, by no means all the talk about him was condemnatory, though the expected points-of-view were present; that is, those who had supported him previously were outraged and now condemned him; those who had previously scorned him, now supported him. But his judgments of concerts and art shows, though completely awry to my eyes, were no less razor-sharp; all his customary incisiveness and invective were present, his keenness of perception seemed not altered save in that he perceived things now, as it were, from a different perspective, a perspective radically altered from his past point-of-view. His opinions were startling and often outrageous.

The magnificent and aging prima donna, Madame Bursa-DeKoyer was "a towering monument to bourgeois taste, which, unfortunately, is not buried under it."

Corydon de Neuvalet, the rage of New York, was "at best an amusing imposter, whose Surrealistic sacrileges are displayed in Fifth Avenue shop windows by shopkeepers whose knowledge of art is somewhat less than an amount necessary to be seen under a microscope, though in his sense of color he is tenth-best Vermeer, even though he never challenges even the least of Ahapi."

The paintings of the insane artist Veilain excited his extravagant admiration. "Here is evidence that someone who can hold a brush and who knows color when he sees it can see more in the world around him than most of the benighted who look upon his canvases. Here is genuine perception, uninhibited by any terrestrial dimensions, unhampered by any mass of human tradition, sentimental or otherwise. The appeal is to a plane which stems from the primitive, yet rises above it; the background is in events of the past and present which exist in conterminous folds of space and are visible only to those gifted with extra-sensory perception, which is perhaps a property of certain people adjudged 'insane'."

Of a concert by Fradelitski of the conductor's current favorite, the Russian symphonist, Blantanovich, he wrote so scathingly that Fradelitski publicly threatened suit. "Blantanovich's music is an expression of that dreadful culture which supposes that every man is the precise political equal of every other, save those who are at the top, who are, to quote Orwell, 'more equal'; it need not be played at all and would not be if it were not for Fradelitski, who is distinguished indeed among conductors, for in the entire world, he is the only one who learns progressively less with each concert he conducts."

It was not to be wondered at that Jason Wecter's name was on every tongue; he was inveighed against, the *Dial* could not begin to publish the letters received; he was praised, complimented, damned, cast out from social circles to which he had hitherto always had invitation, but above all, he was talked about, and whether on one day he was called a Communist and on the other a die-hard reactionary seemed to make no difference to him, for he was seldom seen anywhere but at the concerts he had to attend, and there he spoke to no one. Yet, he was seen at one other place: at the Widener, and later it was reported that he had twice been seen in the rare book collection of Miskatonic University at Arkham.

Such was the situation when, on the night of August twelfth, two days before his disappearance, Jason Wecter came to my apartment in a state which I should have judged at best to have been one of temporary derangement. His look was wild, and his talk even more so. The hour was close to midnight, but the night was warm; there had been a concert, and he had heard half of it, after which he had gone home to study in certain books he had managed to take from the Widener. From there he had come by taxi to my apartment, bursting in on me as I was getting ready for bed.

"Pinckney! Thank heaven you're here! I telephoned, but couldn't get an answer."

"I just came in. Take it easy, Jason. There's a scotch and soda over on the table; help yourself."

He bolted a glass with far more scotch than soda in it. He

was shaking, not just in his hands, and his eyes were feverish, I thought. I crossed and put a hand to his forehead, but he brushed it brusquely away.

"No, no, I'm not sick. You remember that conversation we had—about the carving?"

"Quite clearly."

"Well, it's true, Pinckney. It's all true. I could tell you things —about what happened at Innsmouth when the government took over that time in 1928 and all those explosions took place out at Devil Reef; about what happened in Limehouse, London, back in 1911; about the disappearance of Professor Shewsbury over in Arkham not so very many years ago—there are still pockets of secret worship right here in Massachusetts, I know, and they are all over the world."

"Dream or reality?" I asked sharply.

"Oh, this is reality. I wish it were not. But I have had dreams. Oh, what dreams! I tell you, Pinckney, they are enough to drive a man mad with ecstasy to wake to this mundane world and to know that such outer worlds exist! Oh, those gigantic buildings! Those colossi towering there into those alien skies! And Great Cthulhu! Oh, the wonder and beauty of it! Oh, the terror and evil! Oh, the inevitability!"

I went over and shook him, hard.

He took a deep breath and sat for a moment with his eyes closed. Then he said, "You don't believe me, do you, Pinckney?"

"I'm listening. Belief isn't important, is it?"

"I want you to do something for me."

"What is it?"

"If something happens to me, get hold of that carving—you know the one—and take it out somewhere, weight it, and drop it into the sea. Preferably—if you can make it—off Innsmouth."

"Look, Jason, has someone threatened you?"

"No, no. Will you promise?"

"Of course."

"No matter what you may hear or see or think you hear or see?"

"If you wish."

"Yes. Send it back; it must go back."

"But tell me, Jason—I know you've been pretty cutting in your notices during the past week or so—if anyone's taken it into his head to get back at you. . . ."

"Don't be ridiculous, Pinckney. It's nothing like that. I told you you wouldn't believe me. It's the carving—it's reaching farther and farther into this dimension. Can't you understand, Pinckney? It's begun to materialize. Two nights ago was the first time—*I felt its tentacle!*"

I withheld comment and waited.

"I tell you, I woke from sleep and felt its cold, wet tentacle pulling away the bedclothes; I felt it against my body—I sleep, you know, without any covering but the bedding. I leapt up, I put on the light—and there it was, real, something I could see as well as feel, withdrawing now, diminishing in size, dissolving, fading—and then it was gone, back into its own dimension. In addition to that, for the past week or so I've been able to hear things from that dimension—that fluted music, for instance, and a weird whistling sound."

At that moment I was convinced that my friend's mind had cracked. "If the carving has that effect on you, why don't you destroy it?" I asked.

He shook his head. "Never. That's my only contact with outside, and I assure you, Pinckney, it's not all dark over there. Evil exists on many planes, you know."

"If you believe, aren't you afraid, Jason?"

He leaned toward me with his glittering eyes fixed on mine. "Yes," he breathed. "Yes, I'm horribly afraid—but I'm fascinated, too. Can you understand? I've heard music from outside; I've seen things over there—beside them everything in this world of ours palls and fades. Yes, I'm horribly afraid, Pinckney, but I will not willingly allow my fear to stand between us."

"Between you and who else?"

"*Cthulhu!*" he whispered.

At this moment he raised his head, his eyes far off. "Listen!" he said softly. "Do you hear it, Pinckney? The music! Oh, that wonderful music! Oh, Great Cthulhu!" And he rose and ran from my apartment, an expression of almost beatific bliss on his ascetic features.

That was my last sight of Jason Wecter.

Or was it?

Jason Wecter disappeared on the second day thereafter, or during the night of that day. He was seen by others, though not to talk to, since his visit to my apartment, but he was not seen later than the following night, when a neighbor, coming in late, saw him by the light of his study window, apparently working at his typewriter, though there was no trace of any manuscript to be found, nor had anything been mailed to the *Dial* for publication in his column in that paper.

His instructions in case of any untoward accident clearly called for my "ownership" of the carving described in detail as that of a "Sea God: Ponape Origin"—quite as if he had wished to conceal the identity of the creature depicted there;

so presently, with the sanction of the police, I repossessed my property, and prepared to do with it as I had promised Wecter I would do, though not before I aided the police in substantiating their deduction that none of Wecter's clothing was missing, that he had apparently risen from his bed and vanished stark naked.

I did not particularly examine the carving when I removed it from Wecter's house, but simply put it into my capacious brief-case and carried it home, having already made arrangements to drive to the vicinity of Innsmouth on the following day and throw the object, duly weighted, into the sea.

That was why it was not until the last moment that I saw the revolting change which had taken place. It should be borne in mind that I did not actually see anything in the process of its taking place. But there is no gainsaying the fact that I did on at least two occasions previously carefully examine the carving in question, and one of those times was at the special behest of Jason Wecter to observe fancied alterations which I could not see. And what I did see I must confess to seeing in a rocking launch, while I heard a sound which can only be described as of someone's voice calling my name as from an unfathomable distance, far far away, a voice like that of Jason Wecter, unless the excitement of that moment served to derange my own senses.

It was when I took the already weighted carving out of my brief-case, sitting far out to sea off Innsmouth in the launch I had borrowed, that I was first aware of that distant and incredible sound which resembled a voice calling my name, and which seemed to come from below me, rather than from above. And it was this, I am certain, which halted my action long enough for me to look once again, however fleetingly, at the object in my hands before it was flung forth to sink out of sight beneath the gently rolling waters of the Atlantic. But I have no doubt about what I saw, none whatsoever. *For I held the carving in such a manner that I could not miss the out-flared tentacles of the thing portrayed by that unknown, ancient artist, could not miss seeing that in one of the hitherto empty tentacles there was now clasped the tiny, unclothed figure, perfect in every detail, of a man, whose ascetic features were unmistakably familiar, a miniature of a man which existed in relation to the figure on the carving, in Jason Wecter's own words, recurring with horrible finality there in that boat, "as a seed to a pumpkin"! And even as I flung it forth, it seemed to me that the lips of that miniature man moved in the syllables of my name, and, as it struck the water, and sank below, I seemed to hear that far-away voice like the voice of Jason Wecter, drown my name, horribly gasping and gurgling, with but one syllable enunciated and the other lapped up in the fathomless water off Devil's Reef!*

The Sandwin Compact

I KNOW NOW that the strange and terrible happenings at Sandwin House had their beginnings much farther back than any of us then imagined, certainly farther back than Eldon or I thought at that time. Manifestly, there was no reason to suppose in those early weeks during which Asa Sandwin's time was running out that his trouble grew out of something in a past so remote as to be beyond our comprehension. It was only toward the end of the affair at Sandwin House that terrible glimpses were afforded us, hints of something frightful and awful behind the commonplace events of everyday life broke through to the surface, and ultimately we were enabled to grasp briefly the heart of what lay beneath.

Sandwin House had originally been called Sandwin-by-the-Sea, but its later appellation had soon come to be far more convenient in use. It was an old-fashioned house, old as such houses were old in New England, standing along the Innsmouth road not too far from Arkham: of two stories and an attic, with a deep basement. The roof was many-gabled, with dormer windows rising from the attic. Before the house old elms and maples stood; behind, only a hedge of lilac separated the lawns from the sharp descent to the sea, for the house stood on a high point of land somewhat removed from the highway itself. In appearance it might have seemed a little cold to the casual passer-by, but to me it had always been colored by memories of childhood vacations spent there with my cousin Eldon; it represented relief from Boston, escape from the crowded city. Until the curious happenings that began in the late winter of 1938, I retained my early impression of Sandwin House; even so, it was not until after that strange winter's end that I became aware of how subtly but certainly Sandwin House had changed from the haven of childhood summers to a malign harbor for incredible evil.

My introduction to those curiously disturbing events was prosaic enough; it came in the shape of a telephone call from Eldon as I was about to sit down to supper with my fellow librarians of Arkham's Miskatonic University in the small club of which we were members. I took the call in the club's lounging room.

"Dave? This is Eldon. I want you to run up for a few days."

"Too busy, I'm afraid," I replied. "I'll try to make it next week."

"No, no—now. Dave—the owls are hooting."

That was all; there was nothing more. I returned to the heated discussion in which I had been engaged when I was summoned to the telephone and had actually picked up the threads of that discussion once more when what my cousin had said effected the necessary bridge into the years past, and instantly I excused myself and left for my rooms to prepare for the journey to Sandwin House. Long ago, almost three decades ago, in those carefree days of childhood play, there had been established between us a certain agreement; if ever one of us uttered a certain cryptic sentence, it was to be interpreted as a cry for assistance. To this we pledged ourselves. That cryptic sentence was: *The owls are hooting!* And my cousin Eldon had spoken it.

Within an hour I had arranged for a substitute to take my place in the library of Miskatonic and was on my way to Sandwin House, driving faster than the law permitted. Candidly, I was half amused, half frightened; the pledge as we had made it in those days was serious enough, but it was, after all, a fancy of childhood; that Eldon had seen fit to utter now that cryptic sentence seemed to me evidence of something seriously disturbing in his existence; it seemed to me now rather the last appeal of dire distress than any casual harking back to childhood.

The night descended before I reached Sandwin House; a chill night with frost. A light snow still covered the ground, but the highway was clear. The last few miles to Sandwin House lay along the ocean, so that the drive was singularly beautiful: the moonlight making a wide path of yellow on the sea, and the wind rippling the water so that the entire bosom of the sea sparkled and gleamed as with some inner light. Trees, buildings, hill-slopes broke into the eastern horizon line from time to time, but lessened the sea's beauty not at all. And presently the large ungainly structure that was Sandwin House broke into the skyline.

Sandwin House was dark save for a thin line of light well toward the rear. Here Eldon lived alone with his father and an old servant, though a country woman or two came regularly to clean the place once or twice a week. I drove the car around to one side where an old barn served as a garage, put the car away, took my bag and made my way to the house.

Eldon had heard me. I encountered him in the darkness just beyond the door, his long face touched a little with moonlight, his dressing-gown held closely to his thin body.

"I knew I could count on you, Dave," he said, taking my bag.

"What's up, Eldon?"

"Oh, don't say anything," he said nervously, as if someone might hear. "Wait. I'll tell you in time. And be quiet; let's not disturb father for the time being."

He led the way into the house, going with extreme care down the wide hall toward the stairs, behind which his own rooms were. I could not help noticing the unnatural quiet of the house and the sound of the sea beyond; it struck me then that the atmosphere was faintly eery, but I shrugged away this feeling.

In the light of his room, I saw that my cousin was seriously upset, despite a false air of healthy welcome; my coming was clearly not an end, but only an incident. He was haggard, his eyes were dark and red-rimmed, as if he had not slept for some days, and his hands moved constantly in that excess of nervousness so common to neurotics.

"Now then, sit down; make yourself at home. You've had supper, eh?"

"Enough," I assured him, and waited for him to unburden himself.

He took a turn or two about the room, opened the door cautiously and looked out, before he came back to sit down beside me. "Well, it's about father," he began without preamble. "You know how we have always lived without any visible income, and yet always seemed to have money. That's been for several generations in the Sandwin line, and I've never bothered my head about it. Last fall, however, money was running very low. Father said he needed to go on a journey, and he went. Father seldom travels, but I remembered then that the last time he traveled, almost ten years ago, we were also in dire straits. But when he came back, there seemed again to be plenty of money. I never saw my father leave the house, and I never saw him come back; one day he was gone; another, he was back. It happened the same way this time—and after he was back, there seemed again to be plenty of money available for our use." He shook his head, perplexed. "I confess to you that for some time thereafter I looked through the *Transcript* with utmost care on the lookout for some notice of robbery; but there was none."

"Some business, perhaps," I murmured.

He shook his head. "But that isn't what worries me now. I could forget that if it weren't for the fact that it seems to have some connections with father's present condition."

"Is he ill, then?"

"Why—yes and no. He isn't himself."

"What do you mean?"

"He isn't the father I knew. I can hardly explain myself, and, naturally, I'm upset. I was aware of this for the first time when I learned he had returned and, pausing outside the door of his rooms, heard him talking to himself in a low, guttural voice. 'I've tricked them,' he said to himself several times. There was more, of course, but at the moment I did not listen. I knocked on the door, whereupon he called out harshly and ordered me to return to my quarters until the following day. Since that time he has been behaving with increasing queerness, and of late he has seemed to me definitely afraid of something or someone—I don't know which. And some unusual things have begun to take place."

"What things?" I asked bluntly.

"Well, to begin with—the wet door-knobs."

"Wet door-knobs!" I exclaimed.

He nodded gravely. "The first time father saw them, he had old Ambrose and me on the carpet demanding to know which of us had gone through the house with wet hands. Of course, neither of us had; he dismissed us abruptly, and there was an end to that. But from time to time a door-knob or two would show up wet, and father began to be afraid of finding them so, developing a kind of apprehension I couldn't mistake for something else."

"Go on."

"Then there are, of course, the footsteps and the music. They seem to sound from the air, or from the earth—frankly, I don't know which. But there is something here I don't understand, and something of which father is frankly afraid; so that he keeps more and more to his rooms; he doesn't come out sometimes for days, and when he does, walks with the air of a man momentarily expecting some enemy to pounce upon him, with his eyes for every stray shadow and movement, and no great concern for Ambrose or me or the women who come to clean—though he has not permitted any of these women in his rooms, preferring to keep them clean himself."

What my cousin had said distressed me not so much for my uncle's sake as for his own; indeed, at the conclusion of his narrative, he was almost painfully upset, and I could neither treat what he had told me with the levity I had the impulse to

do, nor with the gravity he seemed to think it merited. I preserved, accordingly, an interested impartiality.

"I suppose Uncle Asa is still up," I said. "He'll be surprised
to find me here, and you won't want him to know you've sent
for me. So I rather think we'd better go on up now."

My Uncle Asa was in every respect his son's opposite; while
Eldon tended to be tall and thin, Asa was squat and heavy, not
so much fat as muscular, with a short, thick neck, and a
curiously repellent face. He had scarcely any forehead; thick,
black hair grew only an inch above his bushy eyebrows, and a
fringe of beard ran along his jaw from one ear to the other,
though he wore no moustache. His nose was small, almost non-
existent, in contrast to eyes so abnormally large that a first
glance from them invariably startled any beholder. In addition to the unnatural size of his eyes, their prominence was
augmented by thick-lensed spectacles which he wore, for in
later years his eyes had grown progressively weaker and he
found it necessary to consult an oculist every six months. His
mouth, finally, was singularly wide and thin; it was not gross
or thick-lipped, as one might have supposed it would be in
one so squat and heavy, but its width was astonishing, for it
was no less than five inches across, so that, what with the
thick shortness of his neck and his deceptive fringe of beard,
it was as if the line of the mouth divided his head from his
torso. He had a strangely batrachian appearance and already
in our childhood we had nicknamed him *The Frog,* because
at that time he bore a facial resemblance to the creatures Eldon
and I often caught in the meadows and swamp across the highway inland from Sandwin House.

At the moment of our entrance to his upstairs study, Uncle
Asa was bent over his desk, hunched in that aspect so natural
to see. He turned at once, his eyes narrowed, his mouth partly
opened; but almost instantly the aspect of sudden fear was
gone, he smiled affably, and shuffled away from his desk toward me, one hand outstretched.

"Ah, good evening, David. I had not thought to see you
before Easter."

"I found I could get away," I replied. "So I came. Besides,
I hear little from you and Eldon."

The old man flashed a quick glance at Eldon, and I could
not help thinking that while my cousin looked older than he
was, my uncle certainly looked less than the sixty-odd years
that were his. He put out chairs for us and immediately engaged me in conversation about foreign affairs, a subject upon
which I found him astonishingly well informed. The easy in-
formality of his manner did much to offset the impression I
had received from Eldon; indeed, I was well on the way to
thinking that some grave mental illness had taken possession
of Eldon, when I received confirmation of my cousin's suspicions. In the middle of a sentence about the problem of
European minorities, my uncle suddenly broke off with his
head cocked a little to one side, as if he were listening for
something, and an expression of mingled fear and defiance
crossed his face. He seemed to have forgotten about us entirely, so complete was his absorption.

For almost three minutes he sat in this manner, while neither
Eldon nor I made any move whatever beyond turning our heads
a little in an effort to hear what he heard. At the moment, however, there was no telling to what he listened; the wind outside

had risen, and the voice of the sea murmured and thundered along the shore; beyond this rose the sound of some nocturnal bird, an uncanny ululation with which I was not familiar; and above us, in the attic of the old house, a kind of rustling was constant, as if the wind were crying through an aperture somewhere into the room.

For the duration of those three minutes, then, no one of us made a move, no one spoke; then abruptly my uncle's face was contorted with rage; he leaped to his feet and ran to the one open window on the east, closing the window with such violence that I thought the glass must surely break. But it did not. For a moment he stood there mumbling to himself; then he turned and hurried back to us, his features as calm and affable as ever.

"Well, goodnight, my boy. I have much work to do. Make yourself at home here, as always."

He shook hands again, a little ceremoniously, and we were dismissed.

Eldon said nothing until we reached his own rooms once more. Then I saw that he was trembling. He sat down weakly and held his head in his hands, murmuring, "You see! I told you how it was. And that's nothing."

"Well, I don't think you need worry about it," I assured him. "In the first place, I am familiar with any number of people who continue to work in their minds while carrying on conversations, and suddenly cease talking when ideas hit them with force. As to the episode of the window—I confess I cannot attempt to explain it, but—"

"Oh, it wasn't my father," said Eldon suddenly. "It was the cry, the call from outside, that ululation."

"I thought—a bird," I answered lamely.

"There's no bird that makes a sound like that; and the migration hasn't begun except for robins and bluebirds and killdeers. It was that; I tell you, Dave—*whatever it is that makes that sound, speaks to father!*"

For a few moments I was too surprised to answer, not alone because of my cousin's sincerity, but because I could not deny that Uncle Asa had indeed conducted himself as if someone had spoken to him. I got up and took a turn about the room, glancing at Eldon from time to time; but it was evident that my cousin needed no belief of mine to confirm his own; so I sat down near him again.

"If we assume that such is the case, Eldon, what is it that talks to your father?"

"I don't know. I heard it first about a month ago. That time father seemed very frightened; not long after, I heard it again. I tried to find out where it came from, but I could learn nothing; that second time it seemed to come from the sea, as it did tonight; subsequently I was positive it came from above the house, and once I could take oath it came from beneath the building. Shortly after that first time, I heard music—weird music, beautiful, but evil. I thought I had dreamed it, because it induced in me strange, fantastic dreams—dreams of some place far from earth and yet linked to earth by some demonic chain—I can't describe them with any degree of justice at all. At about the same time I was conscious of the sound of footsteps, and I swear to you that they came from somewhere in the air, though on a similar occasion I felt them beneath—not a man's steps, but something larger making them. It is at approximately these times that we find wet door-knobs, and the whole house gives off a strange fish-like odor that seems strongest just outside my father's rooms."

In any ordinary case, I would have dismissed what Eldon had said as a result of some illness unknown to him as well as to me, but to tell the truth, one or two things he had said stirred to life chords of memory which had only begun to bridge the abyss between the prosaic present and that past time in which I had become familiar with certain aspects of life on the dark side, so to speak. So I said nothing, trying to think of what it might be I sought in the channels of my memory, but failing, though I recognized the connection between Eldon's narrative and certain ghastly and forbidden accounts hidden in the library at Miskatonic University.

"You don't believe me," he accused suddenly.

"I neither believe nor disbelieve for the present," I replied quietly. "Let's sleep upon it."

"But you *must* believe me, Dave! The only alternative I have is my own madness."

"It isn't so much a matter of belief as it is some reason for the existence of these things. We shall see. Before we go to bed, tell me one thing: do you know whether you alone are affected by these things, or does Ambrose experience them, too?"

Eldon nodded quickly. "Of course he does; he's wanted to leave, but we've been able to dissuade him so far."

"Then you needn't fear for your sanity," I reassured him. "Now, then, for bed."

My room, as always when I stayed in the house, adjoined Eldon's. I bade my cousin goodnight and walked down the hall in the darkness, entering my room with some anxiety about Eldon occupying my thoughts. It was this anxiety which accounted for my slow reaction to the fact that my hand was wet; I noticed this at the moment I reached up to take off my coat. I stood for a moment staring at my gleaming hand before I remembered Eldon's story; then I went at once to the door and opened it. Yes, the outer door-knob was wet; not only was it wet but it gave off a strong smell of aquatic life, that same fish-like odor of which Eldon had only just a few moments past spoken. I closed the door and wiped my hand, puzzled. Could it be that someone in the house was deliberately plotting against Eldon's sanity? Surely not, for Ambrose had nothing to gain by such a course, and so far as I had been able to ascertain over the years, there was no animosity whatever between my Uncle Asa and Eldon. There was no one else who might be guilty of such a campaign of fright.

I got into bed, troubled still, and trying to bridge the distance between the past and present. What was it happened at Innsmouth almost ten years ago now? What was it lay in those shunned manuscripts and books in Miskatonic University? That I must see them, I knew; so I resolved to return to Arkham as soon as possible. Still trying to search my memory for some clue to the solution of the night's events, I fell asleep.

I hesitate to chronicle what took place shortly after I slept. The human mind is unreliable enough at best, let alone in sleep or just after, when the mental processes are clogged by sluggishness resulting from sleep. But in the light of subsequent events, the dream of that night takes on a clarity and reality which I would have thought possible of nothing in the strange half-world of sleep. For I dreamed; I dreamed almost immediately of a great vast plateau in a strange, sandy world, which bore some resemblance to the high plateaus of Tibet or the Honan country I had once visited. In this place the wind blew eternally, and singularly beautiful music fell upon my ears. And yet that music was not pure, not free of evil, for always there was an undercurrent of sinister notes, like a tangible warning of tribulation to come, like the grim fate notes of Beethoven's *Fifth Symphony*. The music emanated from a group of buildings on an island in a black lake. There all was still; figures stood unmoving, strange-faced beings in the guise of men, some curious hybrid Chinese standing as if on guard.

Throughout this dream it seemed as if I moved with the wind high above, a wind that never ceased. How long I was there, I could not say, for I dreamed endlessly; presently I was away from this place, I looked down from high above the sea upon another island where stood great buildings and idols, where again were strange beings, few of them in the guise of men, and again that deathless music sounded. But here also was something more: the voice of that thing which had but recently in time talked to my Uncle Asa—that same weird ululation emanating from deep within a squat building whose cellars must certainly have been inundated by the sea. For only a brief time I looked upon this island, while from somewhere within me I knew its modern name: Easter Island—then I was gone, held above the frozen fastnesses of the far north, looking down upon a secret Indian village where natives worshipped before idols of snow. Everywhere was wind, everywhere music and the sound of that whistling voice like a prolog to terror, a warning of incredible and awful evil soon to flower, everywhere the voice of primeval horror shrouded and hidden beneath beautiful unearthly music.

I woke soon after, unbearably tired, and lay with eyes open staring into the darkness. Slowly I emerged from somnolence, and slowly I became conscious that the air in my room was heavy, laden with the fish-like odor of which Eldon had spoken; and at the same time I was aware of two other things—the sound of retreating footsteps, and the fading ululation I had heard not only in my dreams but in my uncle's rooms only a few hours ago. I jumped from bed and ran to the window, looking eastward; but there was nothing to be known save that the sounds seemed certainly to emanate from the vast ocean beyond. I crossed my room again and went out into the hall; where the smell of aquatic life was much stronger than it was in my room. I knocked gently on Eldon's door and, receiving no answer, entered the room.

He lay on his back, his arms flung out and his fingers working. That he still slept was evident, though at first I was deceived by the whispered words coming from his lips. In the act of awaking him, I paused, hand outstretched, and listened. His voice was for the most part too low in pitch to carry well, but I did catch several words spoken apparently with greater effort to be clear: *Lloigor—Ithaqua—Cthulhu;* these words were repeated several times before I caught hold of Eldon's shoulder and shook him. His awakening was not swift, as it should have been, but sluggish, uncertain; only after a full minute did he become aware of me, but from the moment of that recognition he was his usual self, he sat up, conscious at the same time of the odor in the room, and the sounds beyond.

"Ah—you see!" he said gravely, as if this were all the confirmation I now needed.

He got out of bed and went over to the windows, standing there to look out.

"Did you dream?" I asked.

"Yes, and you?"

We had had substantially the same dreams. Throughout his narrative about his dreams, I became conscious of movement on the floor above: furtive, sluggish movement, carrying with it sounds as of *something wet* sloshing across the floor. At the same time the ululation beyond the house faded away, and the sound of footsteps, too, came to a stop. But there was now present in the atmosphere of the old house such an air of menace and horror, that the cessation of these sounds contributed little to our peace of mind.

"Let's go up and talk to your father," I suggested abruptly.

His eyes widened. "Oh, no—we won't dare disturb him; he's given orders."

But I was not to be daunted; I turned alone and went up the stairs, where I paused to knock peremptorily on Uncle Asa's door. There was no reply. I came to my knees and looked into the room through the keyhole, but I could see nothing; all was dark. But someone was there, for voices came out occasionally; the one was clearly Uncle Asa's—but strangely guttural and rasping, as if it had undergone some vital change; the other was like nothing I had ever heard before or since—a deep, throaty sound, a croaking, harsh voice, somber with menace. And while my uncle spoke in intelligible English, his visitor quite evidently did not. I set myself to listen, and heard first my uncle's voice.

"I will not!"

The unreal accents of the things in the rooms with him

sounded beyond the door. *"Iä! Iä! Shub-Niggurath!"* There followed a succession of rapid mouthings, as if in violent anger.

"Cthulhu will not take me into the sea; I have closed the passage."

Violence again answered my uncle, who seemed, however, to remain unafraid, despite the significant change in the caliber of his voice.

"Nor Ithaqua come in the wind: I can foil him, too."

My uncle's visitor spat a single word: *"Lloigor!"* and there was no reply from my uncle.

I was conscious of a subtle undercurrent of terror, quite apart from the atmosphere of menace that pervaded the old house; this was because I had recognized in my uncle's speech the same words spoken but a few moments ago by Eldon in his sleep, and understood that some malign influence was at work in the house. Moreover, there began to drift back into my mind certain memories of strange narratives brought back across the years from a time when I had delved into the forbidden texts at Miskatonic University: weird, incredible tales of Ancient Gods, of evil beings older than man; I began to dwell upon the terrible secrets concealed in the *Pnakotic Manuscripts*, in the *R'lyeh Text*, those vague, suggestive stories of creatures too horrible to contemplate in the phosaic existence of today. I attempted to shake myself free of the cloud of fear that insidiously overcame me, but there was that in the atmosphere of the house to make this imposible. Fortunately, the arrival of my cousin Eldon did what I myself could not do.

He had crept up the stairs behind me and now stood waiting for some move on my part. I motioned him forward and told him what I had heard. Then we bent to listen together. There was no longer the sound of conversation, but only a sullen, unintelligible muttering accompanied by the growing sound of footsteps, or rather, of sounds which, by their spacing, might have been footsteps, but were made not by any creature familiar to my ears by its sound, but by something which seemed at every step to be walking into a bog; now there was, too, a faint inner trembling in the old house, a strange, unnatural shuddering, which neither decreased nor increased, but continued until the sound of footsteps ceased, fading into the distance.

During all this time no sound had escaped us, but when the footsteps crossed the room behind the door and *went on into space beyond the house,* Eldon caught his breath and held it until I could hear the blood pounding in his temples bent close to mine.

"Good God!" he burst out at last. "What is it?"

I did not trust myself to answer, but had begun to turn slightly to make some kind of reply, when the door opened with a suddenness that left us both speechless.

My uncle Asa stood there; from behind him on all sides came an overpowering smell, as of fish or frogs, a thick miasmic odor of stagnant water so powerful that it brought me close to nausea.

"I heard you," my uncle said slowly. "Come in."

He stepped aside, and we entered his room, Eldon still somewhat reluctant. The windows in the opposite wall were wide open. At first the dim light disclosed nothing, for it was itself as if shrouded in fog, but presently it was evident that something *wet* had been in the room, something that gave off a heavy vapor, for walls, floors, furniture—all were covered with a heavy dew, and here and there on the floor stood pools of water. My uncle did not appear to notice, or, accustomed to it, had forgotten about it; he sat down in his arm-chair and looked at us, motioning us to seats before him. The vapor had begun almost imperceptibly to lift and Uncle Asa's face grew clearer to my eyes—his squat head even deeper in his body now, his forehead gone entirely, his eyes half closed, so that his resemblance to the frogs of our childhood days was marked: a grotesque caricature, horrible in its implications. With only the slightest hesitation, we sat down.

"Did you hear anything?" he asked. But without waiting for an answer, he went on. "I suppose you did. I have thought for some time I must tell you, and now—there may be little enough time left.

"But I may deceive them yet, I may escape them. . . ."

He opened his eyes and looked at Eldon; he did not seem to see me at all. Eldon leaned forward a little anxiously, for it was evident that something troubled the old man; he was not himself, he seemed only half present, with his mind still wandering in some far place.

"The Sandwin compact must end," he said in a guttural voice not unlike that I had heard in the room. "You will remember that. Let no other Sandwin be in bondage to those creatures. Did you ever wonder where our income came from, Eldon?" he asked suddenly.

"Why, yes—often," Eldon managed to reply.

"And it's been that way for three generations; my grandfather and my father before me. My grandfather signed my father away, and my father signed me away—but I shall not sign you away, never fear. This must be its end. So they will not allow me to go naturally as they did grandfather and father, they will take me before instead of waiting. But you will be free of them, Eldon, you will be free."

"Father, what is it? What's the matter?"

He did not appear to hear. "Make no compact with them, Eldon; shun them, avoid them. Evil is their heritage, such evil as you cannot know. These are things you are better without knowing."

"Who was here, Father?"

"Their servant; he did not frighten me. Nor of Cthulhu am I afraid, nor Ithaqua, with whom I have ridden high over the face of the earth, over Egypt and Samarkand, over the great white silences, over Hawaii and the Pacific—but Lloigor, who can draw the body from the earth piecemeal, Lloigor with his twin brother, Zhar, and the horrible Tcho-Tcho people who tend them in the high plateaus of Tibet—of him. . . ." He paused abruptly and shuddered. "They have threatened me with his coming." He took a deep breath. "Let him come, then."

My cousin said nothing, but looked his distress.

"What is this compact, Uncle Asa?" I asked.

"And you will remember," he went on, oblivious to my question, "how your grandfather's coffin was kept shut, and how light it was. There's nothing in his grave, only the coffin; and in your great-grandfather's, too. They took them, they have them, somewhere they have given them unnatural life, a soulless life—for nothing more than our sustenance, the small income we have had and the knowledge they gave us of their hideous secrets. It began, I think, in Innsmouth—my grandfather met someone there, someone who like him *belonged*

to those creatures who came up, frog-like, out of the sea." He
shrugged and glanced once briefly toward the windows on the
east, where now fog glowed whitely and the sound of the sea
rose distantly, the long roll and murmur of water.

My cousin was about to break the silence that had fallen
with another question, when Uncle Asa turned once more to
us and said briefly, curtly, "Enough now. Leave me."

Eldon protested, but my uncle was adamant. By this time I
needed little further enlightenment; the stories I had heard
about Innsmouth, the Tuttle affair on the Aylesbury road, the
strange knowledge concealed in those shunned texts at Miskatonic University—the *Pnakotic Manuscripts*, the *Book of Eibon*,
the *R'lyeh Text*—and, darkest of all, the dread *Necronomicon*
of the mad Arab Abdul Alhazred: all these things revived
long-forgotten memories of potent evil Ancient Ones, elder
beings of incredible age, old gods who once inhabited not
only earth but the entire universe, who were divided between
forces of ancient good and forces of ancient evil, of which
the latter, now in leash, were yet greater in number if not in
power. Most ancient of all, the Elder Gods, the forces of good
were nameless; but weird and terrible names identified the
others—Cthulhu, leader of the elemental water powers; Hastur,
Ithaqua, Lloigor, who led the forces of air; Yog-Sothoth and
Tsathoggua of earth. It was now apparent to me that three
generations of Sandwins had made a hideous compact with
these beings, a compact that promised surrender of soul and
body in return for their great knowledge and security in the
natural life of the Sandwins: but the most ghastly aspect of
this compact was the obvious indication that each generation
swore away the succeeding generation. My Uncle Asa had at

last rebelled, and he now awaited the consequences.

Once more in the hall, Eldon put a hand on my arm and said, "I don't understand."

I shook his arm off almost roughly. "Nor I, Eldon; but I've some idea, and I want to get back to the library and verify it."

"You can't go now."

"No, but if nothing happens for a day or so, I'll go. I'll come back later."

We spent an hour or so in Eldon's room, talking all around the trouble, and listening almost morbidly for evidence of fur- ther activity above; but there was nothing, and presently I returned to bed, almost as ill at ease for the lack of strange sounds and odors, as I had previously been at their happening.

The remainder of the night passed uneventfully, and so did the next day, during all of which my Uncle Asa did not come from his room. The second night passed quietly, also; so that on the following day I returned to Arkham, welcoming the sight of the ancient gambrel roofs and Georgian balustrades as the face of home.

In a fortnight I returned to Sandwin House, but nothing more had happened. I saw my uncle briefly and was astonished at the change in his aspect: he had grown to look more and more batrachian, and his body seemed to have shrunk a little. He made some effort to conceal his hands, but not before I had seen a peculiar transformation there: a curious growth of skin from finger to finger, the significance of which did not at first dawn on me. I asked him once what more he had heard from the visitors of that night two weeks ago.

"I'm waiting for Lloigor," he said cryptically, his eyes fixed beadily on the east windows, and a grimness about his mouth.

In this hiatus, I had learned more about the dread secrets of the Elder Gods and the beings of evil they had long ago banished to the hidden places of earth—the Arctic wastes, the desert land, the shunned Plateau of Leng in the heart of Asia, the Lake of Hali, the vast and remote caverns under the seas. I had learned enough to be convinced of my uncle's hideous compact: the pledge of body and soul to serve the spawn of Cthulhu and Lloigor among the Tcho-Tcho people in remote Tibet, to serve them in after-life in their constant struggle against the domination of the Elder Gods, the seals put upon them by the retreating Ancient Ones, the struggle to rise again and spread horror throughout earth.

That my uncle's father and grandfather were even now so serving in some distant fastness, I could not reasonably doubt, for evidence of evil activity was all about me, not alone in tangible things, but in the incredibly strong aura of intangible terror that held the house in siege. On that second visit I found my cousin somewhat reassured, but still waiting half fearfully for something to happen. I could not stir him to any hope, but must perforce reveal to him some of the things I had verified in the ancient and forbidden books reposing in the vaults of Miskatonic.

On the night preceding my departure, while we sat a little uneasily in Eldon's room waiting for something to happen, the door was suddenly opened and my uncle came in, walking with a strange, halting gait unnatural to him. He seemed somehow to have grown smaller, too, now that I saw him on his feet, and his clothes bagged on him.

"Eldon, why don't you go into Arkham with David tomorrow," he said without preamble. "A little change will do you good."

"Yes, I'd like to have him," I said.

Eldon shook his head. "No, I'll stay to see that nothing happens to you, Father."

Uncle Asa laughed brittlely and, I thought, with a faint sneer, as if to deprecate anything Eldon might attempt to do. If Eldon did not understand his father's attitude, it was clear enough to me, since I knew more than Eldon something of the power of the primeval evil to which my uncle had become allied.

My uncle shrugged then. "Well, you're safe enough; unless you're frightened to death. I don't know."

"You expect something to happen soon, then?" I asked.

The old man gave me a searching glance. "It is clear that you do, David," he said thoughtfully. "I expect Lloigor, yes. If I am able to fight him, I shall be free of him. If I am not—" He shrugged and added, "Then, I think, Sandwin House will be free of this accursed cloud of evil that has shrouded it for so long."

"There is a time?" I asked.

His glance did not waver, but his eyes narrowed a little. "When the full moon rises, I think. If my computations are correct, Arcturus must also be above the horizon before Lloigor can come on his cosmic wind—for, being a wind elemental, he will travel as wind. But I will be waiting for him." He shrugged once more, as if he were dismissing some trivial event instead of the grave threat to his life that was inherent in his words. "Very well, then, Eldon; do as you wish."

He left the room and Eldon turned to me.

"Can't we help him fight this thing, Dave? There must be some way."

"If there is a way, your father knows it."

He hesistated for a long minute before he spoke of something evidently on his mind for some time. "Did you notice father's appearance? How he seems to have changed?" He shuddered. "Like a frog, Dave."

I nodded. "There is some relation between his aspect and that of the creatures with whom he has become aligned. There was something of this in Innsmouth, too—people who bore a strange resemblance to the inhabitants of Devil Reef before the reef was bombed; you must remember it, Eldon."

He said no more until I spurred him on by telling him that he must keep in touch with me by telephone.

"That may be too late, Dave."

"No. I'll come at once. At the first sign of anything amiss, call me."

He agreed, and he went to bed for a restless but quiet night.

The April moon reached its greatest fullness at approximately midnight on the night of April twenty-seventh. Long before that time, I was ready for Eldon's telephone call; indeed, more than once in the late afternoon and early evening hours, I had the impulse to go to Sandwin House without waiting for Eldon to call, but I resisted. At nine o'clock that night, Eldon called; oddly enough, I had just become cognizant of Arcturus standing over the roofs of Arkham in the east, its amber light glowing brightly despite the brilliance of the moon. That something had happened, I knew, for Eldon's voice shook, his words were clipped, he was eager to say what he must so that I could come without delay.

"For God's sake, Dave—come."

He said no more; he needed to say no more. Within a few minutes I was in my car speeding up the coast toward Sandwin House. The night was quiet, windless; killdeers and whippoorwills were calling, and an occasional nighthawk swooped and skycoasted within the glow of my car's lights. The air was fragrant with the smell of growing things, the rich aroma of turned earth and early foliage, of swampland and open water, all in direct contrast to the horror that clung tenaciously to mind.

As before, Eldon met me in the yard at Sandwin House. I had no sooner got out of my car than he was there beside me, greatly distraught, his hands trembling.

"Ambrose has just gone," he said. "He went before the wind started—because of the whippoorwills."

As he spoke, I was conscious of the whippoorwills: scores of them calling from all around, and I remembered the superstition believed by so many of the natives—that at the approach of death, the whippoorwills, in the service of evil, called for the soul of the dying. Their crying was constant, unceasing, rising most steadily and loudly from the meadows west of the Sandwin House, but sounding to some degree all around: a kind of maddening outcry for the birds seemed close, and the cry of a whippoorwill, nostalgic and lonely at a distance, multiplied many times and placed near by, becomes a harsh, shrill call, difficult to tolerate for long: I smiled grimly at Ambrose's flight, and remembered Eldon's saying he had gone before the wind began. The night was windless still.

"What wind?" I asked abruptly.

"Come in."

He turned and led the way swiftly into the house.

From the moment that I stepped across the threshold of Sandwin House that night, I entered another world, remote from that I had just left. For the first thing of which I was cognizant was the high rushing sound of great winds; the house itself seemed to tremble under the impact of tremendous forces from without, and yet I knew, having just come in from outside, that the air was quiet, that no wind blew. The winds, then, sounded within the house, from the upper stories, those quarters occupied by my Uncle Asa, those quarters linked psychically to the incredible evil with which he had become allied. In addition to this incessant rushing of wind, there came as from a great distance that shudderingly familiar ululation, striking in from the east, and at the same time the sound of gigantic footsteps, the soggy, wet footsteps, accompanied by an undeniable sucking noise that seemed to emanate from somewhere beneath us and yet beyond the house itself, beyond even terrestrial earth as we knew it: this, too, arose from some psychic source; this, too, was a manifestation of those evil beings with whom the Sandwins had made the ghastly compact.

"Where's your father?" I asked.

"In his rooms; he won't come out. The door's shut, and I can't go in."

I went up the stairs toward the door to my uncle's quarters with the intention of opening that door by force. Eldon came protestingly behind; it was no use, he assured me; he had tried it and failed. I was almost upon the door when I was stopped in mid-stride by an impassible barrier—no thing of substance, but a wall of cold, chilling air beyond which I could not go, no matter how much I tried.

"You see!" cried Eldon.

I tried and tried again to reach through that impassive wall of air toward the door, but I could not. Finally, in desperation, I called out to Uncle Asa. But no human voice answered me; I was not answered at all save by the roaring of great winds somewhere beyond that door, for, strong as the winds had sounded in the lower hall, in the quarters occupied by my uncle the sound of them was incredibly powerful, and it seemed as if at any moment the walls must fly asunder by the terrific forces that were unleashed there. Throughout all this time, the sound of footsteps and the ululation too were growing in magnitude; they were *approaching* the house from the direction of the sea, if such an occurrence were possible in the light of their seeming already there, a part of the unholy aura of evil in which Sandwin House was cloaked. Simultaneously with the approach of these sounds from the water, there struck into our consciousness another sound from high above us, a sound so incredible, that Eldon looked at me and I at him as if we had not heard aright: it was the sound of music and of voices singing, rising and falling, alternately clear and vague. But in a moment we understood the source of that music as the same from which had come that weirdly beautiful music we had heard in our dreams in Sandwin House; for the music, on the surface of it so beautiful and ethereal, abounded with hellish undertones. It was such music as the sirens might have sung to Ulysses, it was beautiful as the Venusberg music, but perverted by evil that was horribly manifest.

I turned to Eldon, who stood wide-eyed and trembling behind me. "Are there any windows open?"

"Not in father's rooms. He worked at that the past few

days." He held his head cocked to one side and suddenly gripped my arm. "Listen!"

There arose now from beyond the door a growing ululation accompanied by a ghastly gibbering from among which certain words were audible, certain horrible words only too familiar to me from sight of them in those forbidden books at Miskatonic University, the sounds of those creatures bound in unholy alliance to the Sandwins, the evil mouthings of those hellish beings long ago banished to outer spaces, to remote places of earth and universe by the Elder Gods on distant Betelgeuse.

I listened with mounting horror, made all the greater by knowledge of my impotence, and tinged now with a certain nameless fear for my own existence. The mouthings beyond the door mounted in intensity, with occasionally a sharp sound that must have been made by someone different from them. Their own voices were clear, however, rising and falling even as music still sounded distantly, as if a group of servants were singing their adoration for their master, a hellish chant, a triumphant ululation:

"Iä! Iä! Lloigor! Ugh! Shub-Niggurath! . . . Lloigor fhtagn! Cthulhu fhtagn! Ithaqua! Ithaqua! . . . Iä! Iä! Lloigor naflfhtagn! Lloigor cf'ayak vulgtmm, vugtlagln vulgtmm. Ai! Ai! Ai!"

There was a brief lull, during which some voice came as if in answer: a harsh, frog-like croaking of words unintelligible to me: in a voice whose harsh sound still bore some overtones vaguely, arrestingly familiar to me, as if somewhere before I had heard certain of these inflections. This harsh croaking came more and more hesitantly, the gutturals apparently failing the speaker, and then once again rose that triumphant ululation, that maddening chorus of voices from beyond the door, accompanied by such a feeling of dread horror that no words can describe it.

Trembling violently, my cousin held out his arm to show me that his wristwatch indicated but a few minutes before midnight, the hour of the full moon. The voices in the rooms before us continued to rise in intensity, and the wind rose, so that it was as if we stood in a raging cyclone; at the same time the harsh croaking voice resumed again, mounting in intensity until abruptly it changed into the most awful wailing man ever heard, the crying of a lost soul, the demon-ridden scream of a soul lost for all time.

It was then, I think, that realization came to me, that I knew and recognized the harsh croaking voice as not one of my uncle's hellish visitor's at all, but *the voice of Uncle Asa!*

At the moment of this ghastly recognition, which must have come to Eldon at the same time, the sounds beyond the door rose to unbearable shrillness, the demoniac winds thundered and roared; my head whirled; I clapped my hands to my ears— so much I remember, and then nothing more.

I awoke to find Eldon bending over me; I was still in the upper hall, lying on the floor before the entrance to my uncle's quarters, and Eldon's pale, luminous eyes were peering anxiously into mine.

"You fainted," he whispered. "So did I."

I started up, startled by the sound of his voice that seemed so loud, though it had been but a whisper.

All was still. No sound disturbed the quiet of Sandwin House. At the far end of the hall the moonlight lay in a parallelogram of white light, lending a mystic illumination to the darkness all around. My cousin looked toward the door to my uncle's quarters, and I went forward unhesitatingly, and yet afraid of what we might find behind it.

The door was still locked; we had finally to break it down. Eldon struck a match to relieve the deep darkness of the rooms.

I don't know what Eldon expected to find, but what we found was far beyond even my most fearful expectations. Even as Eldon had said, the windows had been boarded up so securely that not a single ray of moonlight penetrated the rooms, and on the sills had been laid a strange collection of five-pointed stones. But there had been one point of entrance my uncle had evidently forgotten: the attic window, though this was closed and locked save for a tiny break in one pane. The course of my uncle's visitors had been unmistakable—a wet trail leading into the quarters from the trap-door near the attic window. The rooms were in frightful condition: no single thing remained intact save the chair in which my uncle habitually sat; it was indeed as if a powerful gale had torn asunder papers, furniture, hangings with equal malevolence.

But it was my uncle's chair to which our attention was directed, and what we saw there was all the more frightful in its significance now that the tangible aura of horror had been removed from Sandwin House. The trail leading from the trap-door and attic window went directly to my uncle's chair and back again: a strange shapeless procession of marks—snake-like, some of them, the prints of webbed feet, which, most curiously, seemed to emanate from the chair in which my uncle had been wont to sit and pass outward: all led back to that tiny break in the pane of the attic window; something had come in and something more had gone out. Incredible, terrible, awful to contemplate—what must have taken place while we lay beyond the door, what must have wrung from my uncle that terrible wailing we had heard before we lapsed into unconsciousness.

For of my uncle there was no trace save one—the ghastly remnants of what stood *for* him, rather than *of* him. *In the chair, his favorite chair, lay his clothes: not taken off and flung carelessly down, not that—but in the horrible, life-like position of a man sitting there, fallen a little together: from cravat to shoes, the terrible mockery of a man sitting there—but they were empty, a shell about which clung an abysmal clothing shaped by some ghastly power beyond our comprehension into the effigy of the man who had worn them, the man who, by all the evidence, was drawn or sucked out of them as by some frightful, malign being who employed in his aid the terrible wind heard within the rooms: the mark of Lloigor, who walks the winds among the star-spaces, the terrible Lloigor against whom my uncle had had no weapon!*

The House in the Valley

I

I, JEFFERSON BATES, make this deposition now, in full knowledge that, whatever the circumstances, I have not long to live. I do so in justice to those who survive me, as well as in an attempt to clear myself of the charge of which I have been so unjustly convicted. A great, if little-known American writer in the tradition of the Gothic once wrote that "the most merciful thing in the world is the inability of the human mind to correlate all its contents," yet I have had ample time for intense thought and reflection, and I have achieved an order in my thoughts I would never have thought possible only so little as a year ago.

For, of course, it was within the year that my "trouble" began. I put it so because I am not yet certain what other name to give it. If I had to set a precise day, I suppose in all fairness, it it must be the day on which Brent Nicholson telephoned me in Boston to say he had discovered and rented for me the very place of isolation and natural beauty I had been seeking for the purpose of working at some paintings I had long had in mind. It lay in an almost hidden valley beside a broad stream, not far from, yet well in from the Massachusetts coast, in the vicinity of the ancient settlements of Arkham and Dunwich, which every artist of the region knows for their curious gambrel structure, so pleasing to the eye, however forbidding to the spirit.

True, I hesitated. There were always fellow artists pausing for a day in Arkham or Dunwich or Kingston, and it was precisely fellow-artists I sought to escape. But in the end, Nicholson persuaded me, and within the week I found myself at the place. It proved to be a large, ancient house—certainly of the same vintage as so many in Arkham—which had been built in a little valley which ought to have been fertile but showed no sign of recent cultivation. It rose among gaunt pines, which crowded close on the house, and along one wall ran a broad, clear brook.

Despite the attractiveness it offered the eye at a distance, up close it presented another face. For one thing, it was painted black. For another, it wore an air of forbidding formidableness. Its curtainless windows stared outward gloomily. All around it on the ground floor ran a narrow porch which had been stuffed and crammed with bundles of sacking tied with twine, half-rotted chairs, highboys, tables, and a singular variety of old-fashioned household objects, like a barricade designed either to keep someone or something inside or to prevent it from getting in. This barricade had manifestly been there a long time, for it showed the effects of exposure to several years of weather. Its reason for being was too obscure even for the agent, to whom I wrote to ask, but it did help to lend the house a most curious air of being inhabited, though there was no sign of life, and nothing, indeed, to show that anyone had lived there for a very long time.

But this was an illusion which never left me. It was plain to see that no one had been in the house, not even Nicholson or the agent, for the barricade extended across both front and back doors of the almost square structure, and I had to pull away a section of it in order to make an entry myself.

Once inside, the impression of habitation was all the stronger. But there was a difference—all the gloom of the black-painted exterior was reversed inside. Here everything was light and surprisingly clean, considering the period of its abandonment. Moreover, the house was furnished, scantily, true, but furnished, whereas I had received the distinct impression that everything which had once been inside had been piled up around the house on the verandah outside.

The house inside was as box-like as it appeared on the outside. There were four rooms below—a bedroom, a kitchen-pantry, a dining-room, a sitting-room; and upstairs, four of exactly the same dimensions—three bedrooms, and a storeroom. There were plenty of windows in all the rooms, and especially those facing north, which was gratifying, since the north light is best for painting.

I had no use for the second storey; so I chose the bedroom on the northwest corner for my studio, and it was there that I put in my things, without regard for the bed, which I pushed aside. I had come, after all, to work at my paintings, and not for any social life whatever. And I had come amply supplied, with my car so laden that it took me most of the first day to unload and store my things, and to clear away a path from the back door, as I had cleared the front, so that I might have access to both north and south sides of the house with equal facility.

Once settled, with a lamp lit against the encroaching darkness, I took out Nicholson's letter and read it once more, as it were, in the proper setting, taking note again of the points he made.

"Isolation will indeed be yours. The nearest neighbors are at least a mile away. They are the Perkinses on the ridge to the south. Not far past them are the Mores. On the other side, which would make it north, are the Bowdens.

"The reason for the long-term desertion is one which ought to appeal to you. People did not want to rent or buy it simply because it had once been occupied by one of those strange, ingrown families which are common in obscure and isolated rural areas—the Bishops, of which the last surviving member, a gaunt, lanky creature named Seth, committed a murder in the house, the one fact which the superstitious natives allow to deter them from use of either the house or the land, which, as you will see—if you had any use for it—is rich and fertile. Even a murderer could be a creative artist in his way, I suppose—but Seth, I fear, was anything but that. He seems to have been somewhat crude, and killed without any good reason —a neighbor, I understand. Simply tore him apart. Seth was a very strong man. Gives me cold chills, but hardly you. The victim was a Bowden.

"There is a telephone, which I ordered connected.

"The house has its own power plant, too. So it's not as ancient as it looks. Though this was put in long after the house was originally built. It's in the cellar, I am told. It may not be working now.

"No waterworks, sorry. The well ought to be good, and you'll need some exercise to keep yourself fit—you can't keep fit sitting at an easel.

"The house looks more islolated than it is. If you get lonely, just telephone me."

The power plant, of which he had written, was not working. The lights in the house were dead. But the telephone was in working order, as I ascertained by placing a call to the nearest village, which was Aylesbury.

I was tired that first night, and went to bed early. I had brought my own bedding, of course, taking no chances on anything left for so long a time in the house, and I was soon asleep. But every instant of my initial day in the house I was aware of that vague, almost intangible conviction that the house was occupied by someone other than myself, though I knew how absurd this was for I had made a thorough tour of the house and premises soon after I had first entered it, and had found no place where anyone might be concealed.

Every house, as no sensitive person needs to be told, has its own individual atmosphere. It is not only the smell of wood, or of brick, old stone, paint—no, it is also a sort of residue of people who have lived there and of events which have transpired within its walls. The atmosphere of the Bishop house challenged description. There was the customary smell of age, which I expected, of dampness rising from the cellar, but there was something beyond this and of greater importance, something which actually lent the house itself an aura of life, as if it were a sleeping animal waiting with infinite patience for something, which it knew must happen, to take place.

It was not, let me say at once, anything to prompt uneasiness. It did not seem to me in that first week to have about it any element of dread or fear, and it did not occur to me to be at all disquieted until one morning in my second week—after I had already completed two imaginative canvases, and was at work outside on a third. I was conscious that morning of being scrutinized; at first I told myself, jokingly, that of course the house was watching me, for its windows did look like blank eyes peering out of that sombre black; but presently I knew that my observer stood somewhere to the rear, and from time to time I flashed glances toward the edge of the little woods which rose southwest of the house.

At last I located the hidden watcher. I turned to face the bushes where he was concealed, and said, "Come on out; I know you're there."

At that a tall, freckle-faced young man rose up and stood looking at me with hard, dark eyes, manifestly suspicious and belligerent.

"Good morning," I said.

He nodded, without saying anything.

"If you're interested, come on up and have a look," I said.

He thawed a little and stepped out of the bushes. He was, I saw now, perhaps twenty. He was clad in jeans, and was barefooted, a lithe young fellow, well-muscled, and undoubtedly quick and alert. He walked forward a little way, coming just close enough so that he could see what I was doing, and there stopped. He favored me with a frank examination. Finally he spoke.

"Your name Bishop?"

Of course, the neighbors might understandably think that a member of the family had turned up in some remote corner of the earth and come back to claim the abandoned property. The name of Jefferson Bates would mean nothing to him. Moreover, I was curiously reluctant to tell him my name, which I could not

understand. I answered civilly enough that my name was not
Bishop, that I was not a relative, that I had only rented the
house for the summer and perhaps a month or two in the fall.

"My name's Perkins," he said. "Bud Perkins. From up yon-
der." He gestured toward the ridge to the south.

"Glad to know you."

"You been here a week," Bud continued, offering proof that
my arrival had not gone unnoticed in the valley. "You're still
here."

There was a note of surprise in his voice, as if the fact of my
being in the Bishop house after a week was strange of itself.

"I mean," he went on, "nothing's happened to you. What with
all the goins-on in this house, it's a wonder."

"What goings-on?" I asked bluntly.

"Don't you know?" he asked, open-mouthed.

"I know about Seth Bishop."

He shook his head vigorously. "That ain't near the all of it,
Mister. I wouldn't set foot in that house if I was paid for it—
and paid good. Makes my spine prickle jest to be standing this
near to it." He frowned darkly. "It's a place should-a been
burned down long ago. What were them Bishops doing all
hours hours of the night?"

"Looks clean," I said. "It's comfortable enough. Not even a
mouse in it."

"Hah! If 'twas only mice! You wait."

With that he turned and plunged back into the woods.

I realized, of course, that many local superstitions must have
arisen about the abandoned Bishop house; what more natural
than that it should be haunted? Nevertheless, Bud Perkins' visit
left a disagreeable impression with me. Clearly, I had been un-

der secret observation ever since my arrival; I understood that new neighbors are always of interest to people, but I also perceived that the interest of my neighbors in this isolated spot was not of quite that nature. They expected something to happen; they were waiting for it to take place; and only the fact that nothing had as yet occurred had brought Bud Perkins within range.

That night the first untoward "incident" took place. Quite possibly Bud Perkins' oblique comments had set the stage by preparing me for something to happen. In any case, the "incident" was so nebulous as to be almost negative, and there were a dozen explanations for it; it is only in the light of later events that I remember it at all. It happened perhaps two hours after midnight.

I was awakened from sleep by an unusual sound. Now, anyone sleeping in a new place grows accustomed to the sounds of the night in that region, and, once accustomed to them, accepts them in sleep; but any new sound is apt to obtrude. Just as a city-dweller spending several nights on a farm may accustom himself to the noises of chickens, birds, the wind, frogs, may be awakened by the new note of a toad trilling because it is strange to the chorus to which he has become accustomed, so I was aware of a new sound in the chorus of whippoorwills, owls, and nocturnal insects which invaded the night.

The new sound was a subterranean one; that is, it seemed to come from far below the house, deep down under the surface of the earth. It might have been earth settling, it might have been a fissure opening and closing, it might readily have been a fugitive tremblor, except that it came and went with a certain regularity, as if it were made by some very large thing moving along a colossal cavern far beneath the house. It lasted perhaps half an hour; it seemed to approach from the east and diminish in the same direction in a fairly even progression of sounds. I could not be sure, but I had the uncertain impression that the house trembled faintly under these subterranean sounds.

Perhaps it was this which impelled me on the following day to poke about in the storeroom in an effort to find out for myself what my inquisitive neighbor had meant by his questions and hints about the Bishops. What had they been doing that their neighbors thought so bad?

The storeroom, however, was less crammed than I had expected it to be, perhaps largely because so many things had been put out on the verandah. Indeed, the only unusual aspect of it that I could find was a shelf of books which had evidently been in the process of being read when tragedy had obliterated the family.

These were of various kinds.

Perhaps chief among them were several gardening texts. They were extremely old books, and had been long in disuse, quite possibly hidden away by an earlier member of the Bishop family, and only recently discovered. I glanced into two or three of these, and found them to be completely useless for any modern gardener, since they described methods of raising and caring for plants which were unknown to me, for the most part—hellebore, mandrake, nightshade, witch hazel, and the like; and such of the pages which were given over to the more familiar vegetables were filled with bits of lore and superstition which held utterly no meaning for anyone in this modern world.

There was also one paper-covered book devoted to the lore of dreams. This did not appear to have been much read, though its condition was such for dust and lint, that it was impossible to draw any conclusions about it. It was one of those inexpensive books which were popular two or three generations ago, and its dream interpretations were the most ordinary; it was, in short, just such a book as one might expect a rather ignorant country-man to pick up.

Indeed, of them all, only one interested me. This was a most curious book indeed. It was a monumental tome, entirely copied in longhand, and bound by hand in wood. Though it very prob-ably had no literary worth whatsoever, it could have existed in any museum of curiosa. At that time I made little attempt to read it, for it seemed to be a compilation of gibberish similar to the nonsense in the dream book. It had a crudely lettered title which indicated that its ultimate source must have been some private old library—*Seth Bishop, His Book :: Being Excerpts from the "Nekronomicon" & the "Cultes des Ghouls" & the "Pnakotic Manuscripts" & the "R'leh Text" Copied in His Own Hand by Seth Bishop in the Yrs. 1919 to 1923*. Underneath, in a spidery hand which did not seem likely for one known to be so uneducated, he had scrawled his signature.

In addition to these, there were several works allied to the dream book. A copy of the notorious *Seventh Book of Moses,* a text much prized by certain oldsters in the Pennsylvania hex country—which, thanks to newspaper accounts of a recent hex murder, I knew about. A slender prayer-book in which all the prayers seemed to be mockeries, for all were directed to Asarael and Sathanus, and other dark angels.

There was nothing of any value whatsoever, apart from being simply curious items, in the entire lot. Their presence testified only to a diversity of dark interests on the part of succeeding generations of the Bishop family, for it was fairly evident that the owner and reader of the gardening books was very probably Seth's grandfather, while the owner of the dream book and the hex text was most likely a member of Seth's father's generation. Seth himself seemed interested in more obscure lore.

The works from which Seth had copied, however, seemed appreciably more erudite than I had been led to believe a man of Seth's background would be likely to consult. This puzzled me, and at the first opportunity I traveled into Aylesbury to make such inquiries as I could at a country store on the outskirts of the village, where, I reasoned, Seth might most probably have made purchases, since he had had the reputation of being a reclusive individual.

The proprietor, who turned out to be a distant relative of Seth's on his mother's side, seemed somewhat loath to speak of Seth, but did ultimately reveal something in his reluctant answers to my persistent questions. From him, whose name was Obed Marsh, I gathered that Seth had "at first"—that is, presumably as a child and young man—been as "backward as any of that clan". In Seth's later teens, he had grown "queer", by which Marsh meant that Seth had taken to a more solitary existence; he had spoken at that time with frequency of strange and disturbing dreams he had had, of noises he had heard, of visions he believed he saw in and out of the house; but, after two or three years of this, Seth had never mentioned a word of these things again. Instead, he had locked himself up in a room downstairs—which had certainly been the storeroom, judging by Marsh's description—and read everything he could lay his hands on, for all that he never "went past the fourth grade". Later on, he had gone into Arkham, to the library of Miskatonic

University, to read more books. After that "spell", Seth had come home and lived as a solitary until the time of his outbreak —the horrible murder of Amos Bowden.

All this, certainly, added up to little save a tale of a mind ill-equipped for learning, trying desperately to assimilate knowledge, the burden of which seemed to have ultimately snapped that mind. So, at least, it appeared at this juncture of my tenure of the Bishop house.

II

That night events took a singular turn.

But, like so many other aspects of that strange sojourn, I was not aware immediately of the full implications of what happened. Set down baldly, it seems absurd that it should have given me any cause for second thought. It was nothing more than a dream which I experienced in the course of that night. Even as a dream, it was not particularly horrifying or even frightening, rather more awesome and impressive.

I dreamed simply that I lay asleep in the Bishop house, that while I so lay a vague, indefinable, but somehow awesome and powerful cloud—like a fog or mist—took shape out of the cellar, billowed up through the floors and walls, engulfing the furniture, but not seeming to harm it or the house, taking shape, meanwhile, as a huge, amorphous creature with tentacles flowing from its monstrous head, and swaying like a cobra back and forth all the while it gave voice to a strange ululation, while from somewhere in the distance a chorus of weird instruments played unearthly music, and a human voice chanted inhuman words which, as I subsequently learned, were written thusly:

Ph'nglui mglw'nafh Cthulhu R'lyeh wgah'nagl fhtagn.

In the end, the amorphous creature billowed even farther upward and engulfed also the sleeper who was I. Thereupon it seemed to dissolve into a long dark passageway, down which came at a frantically eager lope a human being who was certainly similar in appearance to descriptions I had had of the late Seth Bishop. This being grew in size, too, looming almost as large as the amorphous fog, and vanished even as it had done, coming straight at the sleeping figure in the bed in that house in the valley.

Now, on the face of it, this dream was meaningless. It was a nightmare, beyond question; but it lacked any capacity for fear. I seemed to be aware that something of tremendous importance was happening to me or about to happen to me, but, not understanding it, I could not fear it; moreover, the amorphous creature, the chanting voice, the ululations, and the strange music all lent a ritual impressiveness to the dream.

On awakening in the morning, however, I found it readily possible to recall the dream, and I was obsessed with a persistent conviction that all its aspects were not really strange to me. Somewhere I had heard or seen the written equivalent of that fantastic chanting, and, so thinking, I found myself once more in the storeroom, poring over that incredible book in Seth Bishop's handwriting; reading here and there and discovering with wonder that the text concerned an ancient series of beliefs in Elder Gods and Ancient Ones and a conflict between them, between the Elder Gods and such creatures as Hastur and Yog-Sothoth and Cthulhu. This, at last, struck a familiar note, and seeking farther, I discovered what was certainly the chant I had heard—with, moreover, its translation in Seth Bishop's hand, which read:

In his house at R'lyeh dead Cthulhu waits dreaming.

The one disturbing factor in this discovery was that I had most certainly not seen the line of the chant on occasion of my examination of the room. I might have seen the name "Cthulhu", but nothing more in that cursory glance at the Bishop manuscript. How then could I have duplicated a fact which was not part of my conscious or subconscious store of knowledge? It is not commonly believed that the mind can duplicate in a dream state or any other any experience which is utterly alien to it. Yet I had done so.

What was more, as I read on in that often shocking text of queer survivals and hellish cults, I found that hints in vague descriptive passages described just such a being as I had seen in my dream—not of fog or mist, but of solid matter, which was a second occurrence of the duplication of something utterly alien to my experience.

I had, of course, heard of psychic residue—residual forces left behind at the scene of any event, be it major tragedy or any powerful emotional experience common to mankind—love, hate, fear—and it was possible that something of this sort had brought about my dream, as were it the atmosphere of the house itself invading and possessing me while I slept, which I did not regard as completely impossible, since certainly it was strange and the events which had taken place there were experiences of impressive power.

Now, however, though it was noon and the demands of my body for food were great, it seemed to me that the next step in pursuit of my dream lay in the cellar. So to it I made my way at once, and there, after a most exhaustive search, which included the moving away from the walls of tiers of shelves, some still with ancient jars of preserved fruit and vegetables on them, I discovered a hidden passageway which led out of the cellar into a cave-like tunnel, down part of which I walked. I did not go far, before the dampness of the earth underfoot, and the wavering of my light, forced me to return—but not before I had seen the disquieting whiteness of scattered bones, embedded in that earth.

When I returned to that subterranean passageway after replenishing my flashlight, I did not quit it before ascertaining beyond reasonable doubt that the bones were those of animals— for, clearly, there had been more than one animal. What was disturbing about their discovery was not their being there, but the puzzling question of how they had got there.

But I did not at the time give this much thought. I was interested in pushing deeper into that tunnel, and I did so, going as far in the direction, I thought, of the seacoast, as I could before my passage was blocked by a fall of earth. When at last I left the tunnel it was late in the afternoon, and I was famished; but I was reasonably certain of two things—the tunnel was not a natural cave, at least at this end; it was clearly the work of human hands; and it had been used for some dark purpose, the nature of which I could not know.

Now for some reason, these discoveries filled me with excitement. Had I been fully in control of myself, I have no doubt that I would have realized that this in itself was unlike me, but at the moment I was faced and challenged with a mystery which seemed to me insistently of the greatest importance, and I was determined to discover all I could of this apparently hitherto unknown part of the Bishop property. This I could not very well do until another day, and in order to find my way through the cave, I would need implements I had not yet found on the property.

Another trip to Alyesbury was unavoidable. I went at once to the store of Obed Marsh and asked for a pick and shovels. For some reason, this request seemed to upset the old man beyond all reason. He paled and hesitated to wait on me.

"You aimin' to dig, Mr. Bates?"

I nodded.

" 'Tain't none o' my business, but maybe you'd like to know that was what Seth took to doin' for a spell. Wore out three, four shovels, diggin'." He leaned forward, his intense eyes glittering. "And the queerest thing about it was nobody could find out where he was diggin'—never see a shovel-ful of dirt anywhere."

I was somewhat taken aback by this information, but I did not hesistate. "That soil there around the house looks rich and fertile," I said.

He seemed relieved. "Well, if you're aimin' to garden, that's a different thing."

One other purchase I made puzzled him. I needed a pair of rubber boots to shield my shoes from the muck and many parts of the tunnel floor, where, doubtless, the nearness of the brook outside caused seepage. But Marsh said nothing about this. As I turned to go, he spoke again of Seth.

"Ain't heard tell anything more, have you, Mr. Bates?"

"People hereabouts don't talk much."

"They ain't all Marshes," he replied, with a furtive grin. "There's some that do say Seth was more Marsh than Bishop. The Bishops believed in hexes and such-like. But never the Marshes."

With this cryptic announcement ringing in my ears, I took my leave. Prepared now for the tunnel, I could hardly wait for the morrow to come, so that I could return once more to that subterranean place and carry on my explorations into a mystery which must certainly have been related to the entire legendry surrounding the Bishop family.

Events were now moving forward at an increasing tempo. That night two more occurrences were recorded.

The first came to my attention just past dawn, when I caught sight of Bud Perkins lurking about outside the house. I was needlessly annoyed, perhaps, since I was making ready to descend into the cellar; just the same I wanted to know what he was after; so I opened the door and stepped out into the yard to confront him.

"What are you looking for, Bud?" I asked.

"Lost a sheep," he said laconically.

"I haven't seen it."

"It come this way," he answered.

"Well, you're welcome to look."

"Sure hate to think this's all settin' up to start again," he said.

"What do you mean?"

"If you don't know, 'twon't do any good to say. If you do, it's better I don't say a thing, anyway. So I'm not sayin'."

This mystifying conversation baffled me. At the same time, Bud Perkins' obvious suspicion that somehow his sheep had come to my hands was irritating. I stepped back and threw open the door.

"Look in the house if you like."

But at this, his eyes opened wide in positive horror. "Me set foot in there?" he cried. "Not for my life." He added, "Why

I'm the only one's got gumption enough to come this close to the place. But I wouldn't step in there for all the money you could pay me. Not me."

"It's perfectly safe," I said, unable to conceal a smile at his fright.

"Maybe you think so. We know better. We know what's waitin' there behind them black walls, waitin' and waitin' for somebody to come. And now you've come. And now things are startin' up again, jest like before."

With that, he turned and ran, vanishing as on his previous visit into the woods. When I had satisfied myself that he was not coming back, I turned and re-entered the house. And there I made a discovery which ought to have been alarming, but which seemed to me then only vaguely unusual, since I must clearly have been in a lethargic state, not yet fully awake. The new boots I had bought only yesterday for my use had been used; they were caked with mud. Yet I knew indisputably that they had been clean and unused yesterday.

At sight of them, a growing conviction took form in my mind. Without putting on the boots, I descended into the cellar, opened the wall into the tunnel, and walked rapidly to the area of the barrier. Perhaps I had a premonitory certainty of what I would find, for I found it—the cave-in of earth had been dug partially away, sufficiently for a man to squeeze through. And the tracks in the wet earth were clearly made by the new boots I had bought, for the stamped trade-mark in the sole of those boots was plainly to be seen in the glow of my flashlight.

I was thus faced with one of two alternatives—either someone had used my boots in the night to effect this change in the tunnel, or I myself had walked in my sleep to bring it about.

And I could not much doubt which it had been—for, despite my eagerness and anticipation, I was fatigued in a way which would would have been accounted for only by my having spent a considerable portion of my sleeping hours digging away at this blockade in the passageway.

I cannot escape the conviction now that even then I knew what I should find when I pursued my way down that tunnel— the ancient altar-like structures in the subterranean caverns into which the tunnels opened, the evidence of further sacrifice—not alone animals this time, but undeniably human bones, and at the end, the vast cavern opening downward and the faint glimmering far below of waters, surging powerfully in and out through some opening far down, the Atlantic ocean itself beyond doubt, which had made its way to this place by means of sub-surface caverns on the coast. And I must have had a premonition, too, of what else I should see there at the edge of that final descent into the aquatic abyss—the tufts of wool, the single hoof with its portion of torn and broken leg—all that remained of a sheep, fresh as the night just past!

I turned and fled, badly shaken, unwilling to guess how the sheep had got there—Bud Perkins' animal, I felt certain. And had it, too, been brought there for the same purpose as the creatures whose remains I had seen before those dark and broken altars in the lesser caverns between this place of constantly stirring waters and the house I had left not long ago?

I did not tarry in the house long, either, but made my way into Aylesbury once again, apparently aimlessly, but, as I know now, pressed by my need to know yet more of what legend and lore had accumulated about the Bishop house. But at Aylesbury I experienced for the first time the full force of public disap-

proval, for people on the street averted their eyes from me and
turned their backs to me. One young man to whom I spoke hurried past me as if I had not spoken at all.

Even Obed Marsh had changed in his attitude. He was nothing loath to take my money, but was surly in his manner and
obviously wished that I would leave his store as soon as possible. But here I made it clear I would not move until my questions had been answered.

What had I done? I wanted to know, that people should shun
me as they did?

"It's that house," he said finally.

"I'm not the house," I retorted, dissatisfied.

"There's talk," he said then.

"Talk? What kind of talk?"

"About you and Bud Perkins' sheep. About the way things
happened when Seth Bishop was alive." Then he leaned forward with a dark, beetling face, and whispered harshly,
"There's them that say Seth's come back."

"Seth Bishop's dead and buried this long time."

He nodded. "Aye, part of him is. But part of him maybe ain't.
I'll tell you, best thing in the world is for you to clear out now.
You got time yet."

I reminded him coldly that I had leased the Bishop place and
had paid the rent for at least four months, with an option to
complete a year there. He clammed up at once and would say
nothing further about my tenure. I pressed him, nevertheless,
for details about Seth Bishops' life, but all he would or could
tell me was clearly the summation of vague, uncertain hints and
dark suspicions which had been common in the vicinity, so that
I left him at last not with any picture of Seth Bishop as a man

to be feared, but rather of him as a man to be pitied, kept at bay in his black-walled house in the valley like an animal by his neighbors on the ridge and the people of Aylesbury, who were at one in hating and fearing him, without any but the most circumstantial evidence that he had committed any crime against the safety or peace of the environs.

What, in fact, had Seth Bishop knowingly done—apart from the final crime of which he had been proved guilty? He had led a recluse's existence, abandoning even the strange garden of his ancestors, turning his back, certainly, on what was reputed to be his grandfather's and his father's sinister interest in wizardry and the lore of the occult, instead of which he had interested himself obsessively in a far more ancient lore which appeared to be fully as ridiculous as that of witchcraft. One might expect such interests not to falter in such isolated areas, and, in particular, among families so ingrown as the Bishop family was.

Perhaps somewhere in the old books of his forebears Seth had found certain obscure references which had sent him to the library at Miskatonic, where, in his consuming interest, he had undertaken the monumental task of copying great portions of books, which, presumably, he could not get permission to withdraw from the library. This lore which was his primary concern was, in fact, a distortion of ancient Christian legend; reduced to its most simple terms, it was a record of the cosmic struggle between forces of good and forces of evil.

However difficult it was to summarize, it would appear that the first inhabitants of outer space were great beings, not in human shape, who were called the Elder Gods and lived on Betelgeuse, at a remote time. Against these certain elemental Ancient Ones, also called the Great Old Ones, had rebelled—Azathoth,

Yog-Sothoth, the amphibious Cthulhu, the bat-like Hastur the Unspeakable, Lloigor, Zhar, Ithaqua, the wind-walker, and the earth beings, Nyarlathotep and Shub-Niggurath; but, their rebellion failing, they were cast out and banished by the Elder Gods—locked away on far planets and stars under the seal of the Elder Gods—Cthulhu deep under the sea in the place known as R'lyeh, Hastur on a black star near Aldebaran in the Hyades, Ithaqua in the icy Arctic barrens, still others in a place known as Kadath in the Cold Waste, which existed in time and space conterminously with a portion of Asia.

Since this initial rebellion—which was basically in a legend pattern paralleling the rebellion of Satan and his followers against the arch-angels of Heaven—the Great Old Ones had continually sought to regain their power to war against the Elder Gods, and there have grown up on earth and other planets certain cultists and followers—like the Abominable Snowmen, the Dholes, the Deep Ones, and many others, all dedicated to serve the Ancient Ones, and often succeeding in removing the Elder Seal to free the forces of ancient evil, which had then to be put down again either by direct intervention of the Elder Gods or by the alert watchfulness of human beings armed against them.

This was the sum total of what Seth Bishop had copied from very old and very rare books, much of it repetitive, and all surely the wildest kind of fantasy. True, there were certain disturbing newspaper clippings appended to the manuscript—of what happened at Devil Reef off Innsmouth in 1928, of a supposed sea serpent in Rick's Lake, Wisconsin, of a terrible occurrence at nearby Dunwich, and another in the wilds of Vermont, but these, beyond question, I felt to be coincidental accounts which happened to strike a parallel chord. And, while it

was also true that there was as yet no explanation for the subterranean passage leading toward the coast, I felt comfortably
certain that it was the work of some distant forebear of Seth
Bishop's, and only appropriated for his own use at a considerably later date.

All that emerged from this was the portrait of an ignorant
man striving to improve himself in the directions which ap-
pealed to him. Gullible and superstitious he may have been, and
at the end, perhaps deranged—but evil, surely not.

III

It was at about this time that I became aware of a most curious fancy.

It seemed to me that there was someone else in the house in
the valley, an alien human being who had no business there, but
intruded from outside. Though his occupation seemed to be to
paint pictures, I was reasonably certain that he had come to spy.
I caught only the most fugitive glimpses of him—on occasion
a reflection in a mirror or in a windowpane when I was near,
but I saw in the north room of the ground floor the evidence
of his work—one unfinished canvas on his easel, and several
that had been completed.

I did not have the time to look for him, for the One below
commanded me, and each night I descended with food, not for
him, for he devoured what no mortal man knew, but for those
of the deeps who accompanied him, and came swimming up out
of that cavernous pit, and were to my eyes like a travesty born
of men and batrachian things, with webbed hands and feet, and
gilled, and wide, frog-like mouths, and great staring eyes made
to see in the darkest recesses of the vast seas about the place

where He lay sleeping, waiting to rise and come forth once more and take possession again of his kingdom, which was on Earth and in the space and time all about this planet, where once he had ruled above all others until the casting-down.

Perhaps this was the result of my coming upon the old diary, which now I settled down to read, as were it a book I had treasured since childhood. I found it by accident in the cellar, mildewed and showing the effects of having been long lost—a fortunate thing, for there were in it things no outsider should see.

The early pages were gone, having been torn out and burned in an access of fear, before any self-confidence had come. But all the others were still there, and plain to be read in their spidery script . .

"Jun. 8, Went to the meeting-place at eight, dragging the calf from Mores. Counted forty-two of the Deep Ones. Also one other, not of them, which was like an octopus, but was not. Remained there three hours."

That was the first entry I saw. Thereafter the entries were similar—of trips underground to the water pits, of meetings with the Deep Ones and occasionally other water beings. In September of that year, a catastrophe . .

"Sept. 21, The pits crowded. Learned something terrible had happened at Devil Reef. One of the old fools at Innsmouth gave things away, and the Federal men came with submarines and boats to blast Devil Reef and the waterfront at Innsmouth. The Marsh crowd got away, most of them. Many Deep Ones killed. Depth charges did not reach R'lyeh where He lives dreaming . .

"Sept. 22, More reports from Innsmouth. 371 Deep Ones

killed. Many taken from Innsmouth, all those who were given away by the Marsh 'look'. One of them said what was left of the Marsh clan had fled to Ponape. Three of the Deep Ones here tonight from that place; they say they remember how old Captain Marsh came there, and what a compact he made with them, and how he took one of them and married her, and had children who were born of man and the Deep Ones, tainting the whole Marsh clan forever, and how ever since then the Marsh ships fared well, and all their sea enterprises succeeded beyond their wildest dreams; they grew rich and powerful, the wealthiest of all the families at Innsmouth, to which they took their clan to live by day in the houses and by night slipping away to be with the other Deep Ones off the reef. The Marsh houses in Innsmouth were burned. So the Federal men knew. But the Marshes will be back, say the Deep Ones, and all will begin again toward that day when the Great Old One below the sea will rise once more.

"Sept. 23, Destruction terrible at Innsmouth.

"Sept. 24, It will be years before the Innsmouth places will be ready again. They will wait till the Marshes come back."

They might say what they liked of Seth Bishop. No fool, he. This was the record of a self-educated man. All that work at Miskatonic had not been in vain. He alone of all who lived in the Aylesbury region knew what lay hidden in the Atlantic depths off the coast; none other even suspected. . . . . . .

This was the direction of my thoughts, the preoccupation of my days at the Bishop house. I thought thusly, I lived so. And by night?

Once darkness had come to the house, I was more keenly aware than ever that something impended. But somehow mem-

ory rejects what must have happened. Could it be otherwise? I
knew why the furniture had been moved out on the verandah—
because the Deep Ones had begun to come back along the passage, had come up into the house. They were amphibious. They
had literally crowded the furniture out and Seth had never
taken it back.

Each time I left the house to go any distance, I seemed to see
it once again in its proper perspective, which was no longer possible while I occupied it. The attitude of my neighbors was now
quite threatening. Not only Bud Perkins came to look at the
house, but some of the Bowdens and the Mores, and certain
others from Aylesbury. I let them all in, without comment—
those who would come. Bud would not, nor would any of the
Bowdens. But the others searched in vain for what they expected to find and did not.

And what was it they expected to find? Certainly not the
cows, the chickens, the pigs and sheep they said had been
taken. What use would I have for them? I showed them how
frugally I lived, and they looked at the paintings. But one and
all went away sullenly, shaking their heads, unconvinced.

Could I do more? I knew they shunned and hated me, and
kept their distance from the house.

But they disturbed and troubled me, nevertheless. There were
mornings when I woke near to noon, and woke exhausted, as if
I had not slept at all. Most troubling of all, often I found myself
dressed, whereas I knew I had gone to bed undressed, and I
found blood spattered on my clothing and covering my hands.

I was afraid to go back into that subterranean passage by day,
but I forced myself to do so one day, just the same. I went down
with my flashlight, and I examined the floor of that tunnel with

care. Wherever the earth was soft, I saw the marks of many
feet, passing back and forth. Most of them were human footprints, but there were disquieting others—naked feet with
blurred toes, as if they were webbed! I confess I turned the light
away from them, shuddering.

What I saw at the edge of the water pits sent me fleeing
back along the passage. Something had climbed out of those
watery depths—the marks were plain to see and understand,
and what had taken place there was not difficult to imagine, for
all the evidence scattered there in the mute remains which lay
gleaming whitely under the glow of my flashlight!

I knew it could not be long before the neighbors allowed
their resentment to boil over. There was no peace capable of
achievement in that house, nor, indeed, in the valley. Old
hatreds, old enmities persisted, and thrived in that place. I soon
lost all sense of time; I existed in another world, literally, for
the house in the valley was surely the focal point for entry into
another realm of being.

I do not know how long I had been in the house—perhaps
six weeks—perhaps two months—when one day the sheriff of
the county, accompanied by two of his deputies, came grim-
faced to the house with a warrant for my arrest. He explained
that he did not wish to use the warrant, but that nevertheless,
he wished to question me, and if I did not accompany him and
his men willingly, he would have no alternative but to use the
warrant, which, he confided, was based on a serious charge, the
nature of which seemed to him grossly exaggerated and entirely
unmotivated.

I went along willingly enough—all the way to Arkham, in

which ancient, gambrel-roofed town I felt strangely at ease and completely unafraid of what was to come. The sheriff was an amiable man who had been driven to this deed, I had not the slightest doubt, by my neighbors. He was almost apologetic, now that I found myself seated opposite him in his office, with a stenographer to take down notes.

He began by wanting to know whether I had been away from the house night before last.

"Not to my knowledge," I answered.

"You could hardly leave your house and not know it."

"If I walked in my sleep, I could."

"Are you in the habit of walking in your sleep?"

"I wasn't before coming here. Since then, I don't know."

He asked seemingly meaningless questions, always skirting the central point of his mission. But this emerged presently. A human being had been seen in charge of a company of some kind of animals, leading the pack to an attack on a herd of cattle in night pasture. All but two of the cattle had been literally torn to pieces. The cattle had belonged to young Sereno More, and it was he who had made the charge against me, an act in which he was abetted by Bud Perkins, who was even more insistent than Sereno.

Now that he had put the charge into words, it seemed more ridiculous than ever. He himself apparently felt so, for he became more than ever apologetic. I myself could hardly forebear laughing. What motive could I have for so mad an act? And what "animals" could I have led? I owned none, not even a dog or cat.

Nevertheless, the sheriff was politely persistent. How had I come by the scratches visible on my arms?

I seemed to be aware of them for the first time and gazed at them thoughtfully.

Had I been picking berries?

I had, and said so. But I added also that I could not recall having been scratched.

The sheriff seemed relieved at this. He confided that the scene of the attack on the cattle was bordered on one side by a hedge of blackberry bushes, the coincidence of my bearing scratches was bound to be noticed, and he could not ignore it. Nevertheless, he appeared to be satisfied, and, being satisfied that I was no more than I pretended to be, he became somewhat more loquacious; thus I learned that once before a similar event had occurred, with the charge that time being leveled at Seth Bishop, but, like this, it had come to nothing, the Bishop house had been searched, nothing had been found, and the attack was so baseless and unmotivated that no one could be brought to trial on the suspicions, however dark, of the neighbors.

I assured him that I was perfectly willing that my house be searched, and he grinned at this, and told me in all friendliness that it had been searched from roof to cellar while I was in his company, and once again nothing had been found.

Yet, when I returned to the house in the valley, I was uneasy and troubled. I tried to keep awake and wait upon events, but this was not to be. I fell asleep, not in the bedroom, but in the store-room, poring over that strange and terrible book in Seth Bishop's hand.

That night I dreamed again, for the first time since my initial dream.

And once again, I dreamed of a vast, amorphous being, which rose out of the water pit in the cavern beyond the passage under the house; but this time it was no misty emanation, this time it was horribly, shockingly real, built of flesh that seemed to have been created out of ancient rock, a vast mountain of matter surmounted by a neckless head, from the lower edges of which great tentacles writhed and curled, reaching out to singular lengths; this came rising out of the waters, while all around it flowed the Deep Ones in an ecstasy of adoration and subservience, and once again, as before, the weirdly beautiful music which had accompanied it rose, and a thousand batrachian throats called harshly *"Iä! Iä! Cthulhu fhtagn!"* in accents of worship.

And once again came the sound of great footfalls below the house, in the bowels of the earth . .

At this juncture I woke, and to my terror, heard still the subterranean footfalls, and felt the shuddering of the house and the earth in the valley, and heard distantly the incredible music fading away into the depths below the house. In my terror, I ran and burst from the house, running blindly to get away, only to face into still another danger.

But Perkins stood there, his rifle aimed at me.

"Where you think you're goin'?" he demanded.

I stopped running, not knowing what to say. Behind me, the house was silent.

"Nowhere," I said finally. Then, my curiosity overcoming my dislike of this gaunt neighbor, I asked, "Did you hear anything, Bud?"

"We all been hearin' it, night after night. Now we're guardin' our stock. You might as well know it. We don't aim to shoot, but if we have to, we'll do it."

"It's not my doing," I said.

" 'Tain't nobody else's," he answered laconically.

I could feel his animosity.

"That's the way it was when Seth Bishop was here. We ain't sure he's not still here."

I felt a curious coldness come over me at his words, and at that instant, the house behind me, for all its looming terrors, seemed more inviting than the darkness outside, where Bud and his neighbors stood vigil with weapons as lethal as anything I might find within those black walls. Perhaps Seth Bishop, too, had met this kind of hatred; perhaps the furniture had never been moved back into the house because it made a barrier against bullets.

I turned and went back into the house without a further word.

Inside, all was now quiet. There was not a sound anywhere. I had previously thought it somewhat unusual that not a sign of mouse or rat had existed in the abandoned house, knowing how quickly these small animals take over a house; now I would have welcomed the sound of their scampering to and fro or gnawing. But there was nothing, only a deathly, pregnant stillness, as if the house itself knew it was ringed around with grim, determined men armed against a horror they could not know.

It was late when at last I slept that night.

IV

My sense of time was not effective in those weeks, as I have already set down. If my memory now serves me rightly, there was a lull of almost a month after that night. I discovered that, gradually, the guards had been withdrawn; only Bud Perkins remained, and he stayed grimly night after night.

It must have been at least five weeks later when I woke from sleep one night and found myself in the passage below the house, walking toward the cellar, away from the yawning chasm at the far end. What had awakened me was a sound to which I was unaccustomed—a screaming which could have come only from a human voice, far behind me. I listened in cold horror, and yet somewhat lethargically, while the screams of fright rose and fell, and were cut off terribly at last. Then I stood for a long time in that place, unable to move forward or back, waiting for a resumption of that frightening sound. But it did not come again, and at last I made my way back to my room and fell exhausted on my bed.

I woke that next morning with a premonition of what was to come.

And in mid-morning, it came. A sullen, hateful mob of men and women, most of them armed. Fortunately, they were in charge of a deputy-sheriff, who kept them in a semblance of order. Though they had no search warrant, they demanded the right to search the house. In the face of their mood, it would have been folly to deny them; so I made no attempt to do so. I stepped outside and left the door stand open for them. They surged into the house, and I could hear them going through room after room, upstairs and down, moving and throwing things about. I made no protest, for I was stoutly guarded by three men, one of whom was Obed Marsh, the storekeeper from Aylesbury.

It was to him I finally addressed myself in as calm a voice as

I could muster. "May I ask what this is all about?"

"You sayin' you don't know?" he asked scornfully.

"I don't."

"Jared More's boy disappeared last night. Walkin' home from a school party up the road a piece. He had to come by here."

There was nothing I could say. It was patent that they believed the boy had vanished into this house. However much I wanted to protest, I could not rid my thoughts of the memory of that terrible screaming I had heard in the tunnel. I did not know who had screamed, and I knew now that I did not want to learn. I felt reasonably sure that they would not find the entrance to the tunnel, for it was artfully concealed behind shelving in that small cellar space, but from that moment forward I stood in an agony of suspense, for I had little doubt about what would happen to me if by some chance anything belonging to the missing boy should be found on the premises.

But again a merciful Providence intervened to prevent any discovery—if there were one to be made; I dared to hope that my own fears were groundless. In truth, I did not know, but horrible doubts were now beginning to assail me. How came I in the tunnel? And whence? When I had awakened, I had been on the way back from the water's edge. What had I done there —and *had I left anything behind?*

By twos and threes, the mob came out of the house again, empty-handed. They were no less sullen, no less angry—but they were somewhat dubious and bewildered. If they had expected to find anything, they were sharply disappointed. If the missing boy had not been taken to the Bishop house, they could not imagine where he might have gone.

Urged by the deputy-sheriff, who had given them their way, they now drew back from the house and began to disperse, all but Bud Perkins and a handful of equally grim men, who remained on guard.

Then for days I was aware of the oppressive hatred which was directed toward the Bishop house and its lone occupant.

Thereafter came an interval of comparative quiet.

And then that final catastrophic night!

It began with faint intimations of something stirring below. I suppose I was subconsciously aware of movement even before I was conscious of it. At the time I was reading in that hellish manuscript book of Seth Bishop's—a page devoted to the minions of Great Cthulhu, the Deep Ones who devoured sacrifice of warm-blooded animals, being themselves cold-blooded, and waxing fat and strong on what would seem a kind of pagan cannibalism; I was reading this, I say, when without warning I became conscious of the stirrings below, as if the very earth were becoming animated, trembling faintly, rhythmically, and there began immediately thereafter a faint, far-away music, exactly similar to that which I had heard in my first dream in that house, rising from instruments unknown to human hands, but resembling a fluting or piping sound heard in chorus, and accompanied once more by an occasional ululation which came from the throat of some living entity.

I cannot adequately describe the effect which this had on me. At the moment, engrossed as I was in an account clearly related to the events of the past weeks, I was, as it were, conditioned to such an occurrence, but my state of mind was one of nothing short of exaltation, and I was filled with a compelling urgence to rise and serve Him who lay dreaming far below. Almost as in a dream, I put out the light in the store-room, and slipped out in darkness, possessed by caution against the enemies who waited beyond the walls.

As yet, the music was too faint to be heard outside the house. I had no way of knowing how long it would remain so faint; so I made haste to do that which was expected of me before the enemy could be warned that the dwellers in the watery chasm below were once again rising toward the house in the valley. But it was not to the cellar that I moved. As if by pre-ordained plan, I slipped out the back door of the house and made my way stealthily in the darkness to the protecting shrubbery and trees.

There I began to make slow but steady progress forward. Somewhere up ahead Bud Perkins stood on guard . . . . .

Of what happened after that, I cannot be sure.

The rest was nightmare, certainly. Before I reached Bud Perkins, two shots rang out. That was his signal to the others to come. I was less than a foot away from him in the darkness, and his shots startled me out of my wits. He, too, had heard the sounds from below, for now I could hear them outside in this darkness as well.

So much I remember with reasonable clarity.

It was what happened after that that baffles me even now. Certainly the mob came, and if the men from the sheriff's office had not been waiting, too, I would not now be alive to make this deposition. I remember the screaming, furious mob; I remember that they set fire to the house. I had been back there, I had run out, escaping the flames. From where I looked back, I saw not only the flames, but that other sight—those shrilly crying Deep Ones, falling victim to flame and terror, and at the last that gigantic being which reared up out of the flames flailing its tentacles, before it dropped defiantly back down, compacting into a great sinuous column of flesh, and vanished without trace! It was then that someone in the mob threw dynamite into the flaming house. But even before the echo of the blast had died away, I heard, as did all the others encircling all that remained of the Bishop house, that chanting voice which cried, "*Ph'nglui mglw'nafh Cthulhu R'lyeh wgah'nagl fhtagn!*" —announcing to all the world that Great Cthulhu still lay dreaming in his subequeous haven of R'lyeh!

They said of me that I was crouched beside the torn remains of Bud Perkins, and they intimated hideous things. Yet they 1ust have seen, even as I saw, what writhed in that flaming ruin, though they deny that there was anything at all there but myself. What they say I was doing is too horrible to repeat. It is the fiction of their diseased, hatefilled brains, for surely they cannot deny the evidence of their own senses. They witnessed against me in court, and sealed my doom.

Surely they must understand that it was not I who did all the things they say I did! Surely they must know that it was the life-force of Seth Bishop, which invaded and took possession of me, which again restored that unholy link to those creatures of the deeps, bringing them their food, as in the days when Seth Bishop had an existence in a body of his own and served them, even as the Deep Ones and those countless others scattered over the face of the earth, Seth Bishop who did what they say I did to Bud Perkins' sheep and Jared More's boy and all those missing animals and finally to Bud Perkins himself, for all that he made them believe it was I, for I could not have done such things, it was Seth Bishop come back from hell to serve again those hideous beings who came to his watery pit from the depths of the sea, Seth Bishop, who had discovered their existence and summoned them to do his bidding and who lived to serve them in his own time and in mine, and who may still lurk deep in earth below that place where the house stood in the valley, waiting for another vessel to inhabit and so serve them in time to come, forever.

The Seal of R'lyeh

MY PATERNAL GRANDFATHER, whom I never saw except in a darkened room, used to say of me to my parents, "Keep him away from the sea!" as if I had some reason to fear water, when, in fact, I have always been drawn to it. But those born under one of the water signs—mine is Pisces—have a natural affinity for water, so much is well known. They are said to be psychic, too, but that is another matter, perhaps. At any rate, that was my grandfather's judgment; a strange man, whom I could not have described to save my soul—though that, in the light of day, is an ambiguity indeed! That was before my father was killed in an automobile accident, and afterward it was never said in vain, for my mother kept me back in the hills, well away from the sight and sound and the smells of the sea.

But what is meant to be will be. I was in college in a midwestern city when my mother died, and the week after that, my Uncle Sylvan died, too, leaving everything he had to me. Him I had never seen. He was the eccentric one of the family, the queer one, the black sheep; he was known by a variety of names, and disparaged in all of them, except by my grandfather, who did not speak of him at all without sighing. I was, in fact, the last of my grandfather's direct line; there was a great-uncle living somewhere—in Asia, I always understood, though what

he did there no one seemed to know, except that it had something to do with the sea, shipping, perhaps—and so it was only
natural that I should inherit my Uncle Sylvan's places.

For he had two, and both, as luck would have it, were on the
sea, one in a Massachusetts town called Innsmouth, and the
other isolated on the coast well above that town. Even after
the inheritance taxes, there was enough money to make it un-
necessary for me to go back to college, or to do anything I had
no mind to do, and the only thing I had a mind to do was that
which had been forbidden me for these twenty-two years, to go
to the sea, perhaps to buy a sailboat or a yacht or whatever I
liked.

But that was not quite the way it was to be. I saw the lawyer
in Boston and went on to Innsmouth. A strange town, I found
it. Not friendly, though there were those who smiled when they
learned who I was, smiled with a strange, secretive air, as if they
knew something they would not say of my Uncle Sylvan. Fortunately, the place at Innsmouth was the lesser of his places; it
was plain that he had not occupied it much; it was a dreary,
somber old mansion, and I discovered, much to my surprise, that
it was the faimly homestead, having been built by my great-
grandfather, who had been in the China trade, and lived in by
my grandfather for a good share of his life, and the name of
Phillips was still held in a kind of awe in that town.

No, it was the other place in which my Uncle Sylvan had
spent most of his life. He was only fifty when he died, but he
had lived much like my grandfather; he had not been seen about
much, being seldom away from that darkly overgrown house
which crowned a rocky bluff on the coast above Innsmouth. It
was not a lovely house, not such a one as would call to the lover

of beauty, but it had its own attraction, nevertheless, and I felt
it at once. I thought of it as a house that belonged to the sea,
for the sound of the Atlantic was always in it, and trees shut it
from the land, while to the sea it was open, its wide windows
looking ever east. It was not an old house, like that other—
thirty years, I was told—though it had been built by my uncle
himself on the site of a far older house that had belonged to my
great-grandfather, too.

It was a house of many rooms, but of them all the great central study was the only room to remember. Though all the rest
of the house was of one storey, rambling away from that central
room, that room had the height of two storeys, and was sunken
besides, with its walls covered with books and all manner of
curios, particularly outré and suggestive carvings and sculptures,
paintings and masks which came from many places of the world,
but especially from the Polynesias, from Aztec, Maya, and Inca
country, and from ancient Indian tribes in the northwest coastal
areas of the North American continent—a fascinating and ever
provocative collection which had originally been begun by my
grandfather, and continued and added to by my Uncle Sylvan.
A great hand-made rug, bearing a strange octopoid design,
covered the center of the floor, and all the furniture in the room
was set between the walls and the center of it; nothing at all
stood on that rug.

There was above all else a symbolization in the décor of the
house. Here and there, woven into rugs—beginning with that
great round rug in the central room—into hangings, on placques
—was a design which seemed to be of a singularly perplexing
seal, a round, disc-like pattern bearing on it a crude likeness of
the astronomical symbol of Aquarius, the water-carrier—a like-

ness that might have been drawn remote ages ago, when the shape of Aquarius was not as it is today,—surmounting a hauntingly indefinite suggestion of a buried city, against which, in the precise center of the disc, was imposed an indescribable figure that was at once icthyic and saurian, simultaneously octopoid and semihuman, which, though drawn in miniature, was clearly intended to represent a colossus in someone's imagination. Finally, in letters so fine that the eye could hardly read them, the disc was ringed round with meaningless words in a language I could not read, though far down inside of me it seemed to strike a common chord—*Ph'nglui mglw'nafh Cthulhu R'lyeh wgah'nagl fhtagn*.

That this curious design should have exercised upon me from the beginning the strongest possible attraction did not seem at all strange, though its significance did not come to me until later. Nor could I account for the unimaginably strong pull of the sea; though I had never before set foot in this place, I had the most vivid impression of having returned home. Never, in all my years, had my parents taken me east; I had not before been east of Ohio, and the closest I had come to any substanial body of water had been in brief visits to Lake Michigan or Lake Huron. That this undeniable attraction existed so patently I laid quite naturally to ancestral memory—had not my forebears lived by the sea, on it and beside it? For how many generations? Two of which I knew, and perhaps more before that. They had been mariners for generations, until something happened that caused my grandfather to strike far insland, and to shun the sea thereafter, and cause it to be shunned by all who came after him.

I mention this now because its meaning comes clear in all that happened afterward, which I am dedicated to setting down before I am gone to be among my own people again. The house and the sea drew me; together they were home, and gave more meaning to that word even than the haven I had shared so fondly with my doting parents only a few years before. A strange thing—and yet, stranger still, I did not think it so at the time; it seemed the most natural occurrence, and I did not question it.

Of what manner of man my Uncle Sylvan was, I had no way of knowing at once. I did find an early portrait of him, done by an amateur photographer. It was a likeness of an unusually grave young man, surely not more than twenty, to judge by his appearance, and of an aspect which, while not exactly unattractive, was doubtless repellent to many people, for he had a face which suggested something more than just the humanness of him—with his somewhat flat nose, his very wide mouth, his strangely basilisk eyes. There was no more recent photograph of him, but there were people who remembered him from the years when he still walked or drove into Innsmouth to shop, as I learned on a day I stopped into Asa Clarke's store to buy my supplies for the week.

"Ye're a Phillips?" asked the aged proprietor.

I admitted that I was.

"Son of Sylvan?"

"My uncle never married," I said.

"We've had naught but his word for that," he replied. "Then ye'll be Jared's son. How is he?"

"Dead."

The old man shook his head. "Dead, too, eh?—the last of that generation, then. And you . . ."

"I'm the last of mine."

"The Phillipses were once high and mighty hereabouts. An old family—but ye'll know it."

I said I did not. I had come from the midwest, and had little-knowledge of my forebears.

"That so?" He gazed at me for a moment almost in disblief. "Well, the Phillipses go back about as far as the Marshes. The two were in business long ago, together. China trade. Shipped from here and Boston for the Orient—Japan, China, the islands —and they brought back—" But here he stopped, his face paled a little, and he shrugged. "Many things. Aye, many things indeed." He gave me a baffling look. "Ye figurin' to stay here-abouts?"

I told him I had inherited and moved into my uncle's place on the coast. I was now looking for servants to staff it.

"Ye'll not find 'em," he said, shaking his head. "The place is too far up the coast, and much disliked. If any more of the Phillipses were left—" He spread his hands helplessly. "But most of them died in '28, that time of the explosions and the fire. Still, ye might find a Marsh or two who'd do for you; they're still about. Not so many of 'em died that night."

With this oblique and mystifying reference I was not then concerned. My first thought was of someone to help me at my uncle's house. "Marsh," I repeated. "Can you name one and give me his address?"

"There is one," he said thoughtfully, and then smiled, as if to himself.

That was how I came to meet Ada Marsh.

She was twenty-five, but there were days when she looked much younger, and other days when she looked older. I went to her home, found her, asked her to come to work for me days. She had a car of her own, even if but an old-fashioned Model T; she could drive up and back; and the prospect of working in what she called strangely, "Sylvan's hiding," seemed to appeal to her. Indeed, she seemed almost eager to come, and promised to come that day still, if I wished her to. She was not a good-looking girl, but, like my uncle, she was strangely attractive to me, however much she may have turned others away; there was a certain charm about her wide, flat-lipped mouth, and her eyes, which were undeniably cold, seemed often very warm to me.

She came the following morning, and it was plain to me that she had been in the house before, for she walked about as if she knew it.

"You've been here before!" I challenged her.

"The Marshes and the Phillipses are old friends," she said, and looked at me as if I must have known. And indeed, I felt at that moment as if I did certainly know it was just as she said. "Old, old friends—as old, Mr. Phillips, as the earth itself is old. As old as the water-carrier and the water."

She too was strange. She had been here, as a guest of Uncle Sylvan, I found out, more than once. Now, without hesitation, she had come to work for me, and with such a curious simile on her lips—"as old as the water-carrier and the water"—which made me to think of the design which lay all about us, and for the first time, I now believe, thinking back upon it, implanting in me a certain feeling of uneasiness; for the second moment of it was but a few words away.

"Have you heard, Mr. Phillips?" she asked then.

"Heard what?" I asked.

"If you had heard, you would not need to be told."

But her real purpose was not to come to work for me, I soon found out; it was to have access to the house, as I learned when I came back up from the beach ahead of schedule, and found her engrossed not in work, but in a systematic and detailed search of the great central room. I watched her for a while— how she moved books, leafed through them; how she carefully lifted the pictures on the walls, the sculptures on the shelves, looking into every place where something might be hidden. I went back and slammed the door then; so that when I walked into the study, she was at work dusting, quite as if she had never been at anything else.

It was my impulse to speak, but I foresaw that it would not do to tip my hand. If she sought something, perhaps I could find it first. So I said nothing, and that evening, after she had gone, I took up where she had stopped, not knowing what to look for, but being able to estimate something of its size by the very fact of the places into which she had looked. Something compact, small, hardly larger than a book itself.

Could it be a book? I asked myself repeatedly that night.

For, of course, I found nothing, though I sought until midnight, and gave up only when I was exhausted, satisfied that I had gone farther in my search than Ada could go on the morrow, even if she had most of the day. I sat down to rest in one of the overstuffed chairs ranged close to the walls in that room, and there had my first hallucination—I call it so for want of a better, more precise word. For I was far from sleep when I heard a sound that was like nothing so much as the susurrus of some great beast's breathing; and, wakened in a trice, was sure that the house itself, and the rock on which it sat, and the sea lapping at the rocks below were at one in breathing, like various parts of one great sentient being, and I felt as I had often felt when looking at the paintings of certain contemporary artists—Dale Nichols in particular—who have seen earth and the contours of the land as representative of a great sleeping man or woman—felt as if I rested on chest or belly or forehead of a being so vast I could not comprehend its vastness.

I do not remember how long the illusion lasted. I kept thinking of Ada Marsh's question, "Have you heard?" Was it this she meant? For surely the house and the rock on which it stood were alive, and as restless as the sea that flowed away to the horizon to the east. I sat experiencing the illusion for a long time. Did the house actually tremble as if in respiration? I believed it did, and at the time I laid it to some flaw in its structure, and accounted in its strange movement and sounds for the reluctance of other natives to work for me.

On the third day I confronted Ada in the midst of her search.

"What are you looking for, Ada?" I asked.

She measured me with the utmost candor, and decided that I had seen her thus before.

"Your uncle was in search of something I thought maybe he had found. I too am interested in it. Perhaps you would be, too, if you know. You are like us—you are one of us—of the Marshes and the Phillipses before you."

"What would it be?"

"A notebook, a diary, a journal, papers . . ." She shrugged. "Your uncle spoke very little of it to me, but I know. He was gone very often, long periods at a time. Where was he then? Perhaps he had reached his goal. For he never went away by road."

"Perhaps I can find it."

She shook her head. "You know too little. You are like . . . an outsider."

"Will you tell me?"

"No. Who speaks so to one too young to understand? No, Mr. Phillips, I will say nothing. You are not ready."

I resented this, and I resented her. Yet I did not ask her to leave. Her attitude was a provocation and a challenge.

II

Two days later I came upon that which Ada Marsh sought. My Uncle Sylvan's papers were concealed in a place where Ada Marsh had looked first—behind a shelf of curious, occult books, but set into a secret recess there, which I happened to open only by clumsy chance. A journal of sorts, and many scraps and sheets of paper, covered with tiny script in what I recognized as my uncle's hand. I took them at once to my own room and locked myself in, as if I feared that at this hour, at dead of night, Ada Marsh might come for them. An absurd thing to do —for I not only did not fear her, but actually was drawn to her far more than I would have dreamed I might be when first I met her.

Beyond question, the discovery of the papers represented a turning point in my existence. Say that my first twenty-two years were static, on a waiting plane; say that the early days at my Uncle Sylvan's coast house were a time of suspension between that earlier plane and that which was to come; the turning point came surely with my discovery—and yes, reading—of the papers.

But what was I to make of the first paragraph on which I gazed?

"Subt. Cont. shelf. Northernmost end at Inns., stretching all the way around to vic. Singapore. Orig. source off Ponape? A. suggests R. in Pacific, vic. of Ponape; E. holds R. nr. Inns. Maj. writers suggest it in depths. Could R. occupy entire Cont. shelf from Inns. to Singapore?"

That was the first. The second was even more baffling.

"C. who waits dreaming in R. is all in all, and everywhere. He is in R. at Inns. and at Ponape, he is among the islands and in the depths. How are the Deep Ones related? And where did Obad. and Cyrus make the first contact? Ponape or one of the lesser islands? And how? On land or in the water?"

But my uncle's papers were not alone in that treasure trove. There were other, even more disturbing revelations. The letter, for instance, from the Rev. Jabez Lovell Phillips to some un-named person, dated over a century before, in which he wrote:

"On a certain day in August of 1797, Capt. Obadiah Marsh, accompanied by his First Mate Cyrus Alcott Phillips, reported their ship, the *Cory*, lost with all hands in the Marquesas. The Captain and his First Mate arrived in Innsmouth harbor in a rowboat, yet did not seem any the worse for weather or wear, despite having covered a distance of many thousands of miles in a craft deemed well nigh impossible of having carried them so far. Thereafter began in Innsmouth such a series of happen-ings as were to make the settlement accursed within one genera-tion, for a strange race was born to the Marshes and the Phil-lipses, a blight was fallen upon their families which followed after the appearance of women—and how came they there?—who were the wives of the Captain and his First Mate, and loosed upon Innsmouth a spawn of Hell that no man has found it possible to put down, and against whom all the appeals to Heaven I have made no avail.

"What disports in the waters off Innsmouth in the late hours of darkness? Mermaids, say some. Faugh, what idiocy! Mermaids, indeed. What, if not the accursed spawn of the Marsh and Phillips tribes. . . ."

Of this I read no more, being curiously shaken. I turned next to my uncle's journal, and found the last entry:

"R. is as I thought. Next time I shall see C. himself, where he lies in the depths, waiting upon the day to come forth once more."

But there had been no next time for Uncle Sylvan—only death. There were entries before this one, many of them; clearly, my uncle wrote of matters beyond my knowledge. He wrote of Cthulhu and R'lyeh, of Hastur and Lloigor, of Shub-Niggurath and Yog-Sothoth, of the Plateau of Leng, of the *Sussex Fragments* and the *Necronomicon*, of the Marsh Drift and the Abominable Snowmen—but, most often of all, he wrote of R'lyeh, and of Great Cthulhu—the "R." and the "C." of his papers—and of his abiding search for them, for my uncle, as was made plain in his own handwriting, was in search of these places or beings, I could hardly distinguish one from the other in the way he set down his thoughts, for his notes and his journal were written for no other eyes but his own, and he alone understood them, for I had no frame of reference upon which to draw.

There was, too, a crude map drawn by some hand before my Uncle Sylvan's, for it was old and badly creased; it fascinated me, though I had no genuine understanding of its real worth. It was a rough map of the world—but not of that world I knew or had learned about in my studies; rather of a world that existed only in the imagination of him who had made the map. For deep in the heart of Asia, for instance, the mapmaker had fixed the "Pl. Leng," and, above this, near what ought to have been Mongolia, "Kadath in the Cold Waste," which was specified as "in space-time continua; coterminous," and in the sea about the Polynesians, he had indicated the "Marsh drift," which, I gathered, was a break in the ocean floor. Devil Reef off Innsmouth was indicated, too, and so was Ponape—these were recognizable; but the majority of place-names on that fabulous map were utterly alien to me.

I hid the things I had found where I was sure Ada Marsh would not think of looking for them, and I returned, late though the hour was, to the central room. And there I sought out, as if by instinct, unerringly, the shelf behind which the things I had found had been concealed. There were some of the things mentioned in Uncle Sylvan's notes—the *Sussex Fragments*, the *Pnakotic Manuscripts*, the *Cultes des Goules*, by the Comte d'Erlette, the *Book of Eibon*, Von Junzt's *Unaussprechlichen Kulten*, and many others. But alas! most of them were in Latin or Greek, which I could not read well, however ably I could struggle through French or German. Yet I found enough in those pages to fill me with wonder and terror, with horror and a strangely exhilarating excitement, as if I had realized that my Uncle Sylvan had bequeathed me not only his house and property, but his quest and the lore of aeons before the time of man.

For I sat reading until the morning sun invaded the room and paled the lamps I had lit—reading about the Great Old Ones, who were first among the universes, and the Elder Gods, who fought and vanquished the rebellious Ancient Ones—who were Great Cthulhu, the water-dweller; Hastur, who reposed at the Lake of Hali in the Hyades; Yog-Sothoth, the All-in-One and

One-in-All; Ithaqua, the Wind-Walker; Lloigor, the Star-Treader; Cthugha, who abides in fire; great Azathoth—all of whom had been vanquished and exiled to outer spaces against the coming of another day in far time yet to come, when they could rise with their followers and once again vanquish the races of mankind and challenge the Elder Gods; of their minions —the Deep Ones of the seas and the watery places on Earth, the Dholes, the Abominable Snowmen of Tibet and the hidden Plateau of Leng, the Shantaks, who flew from Kadath in the Cold Waste at the bidding of Wind-Walker, the Wendigo, cousin of Ithaqua; of their rivalries, one and yet divided. I read all this and more—damnably more: the collection of newspaper clippings of inexplicable happenings, accounted for by my Uncle Sylvan as evidence of the truth in which he believed. And in the pages of these books was more of the curious language I had found woven into the decorations of my uncle's house— *Ph'nglui mglw'nafh Cthulhu R'lyeh wgah'nagl fhtagn,*—which was translated, I read in more than one of these accounts, as: "In his house at R'lyeh, dead Cthulhu lies dreaming . . ."

And my uncle's quest was surely nothing more than to find R'lyeh, the sunken subaqueous place of Cthulhu!

In the cold light of day, I challenged my own conclusions. Could my Uncle Sylvan have believed in such a panoply of myths? Or was his pursuit merely the quest of a man steeped in idleness? My uncle's library consisted of many books, ranging through the world's literature; yet one considerable section of his shelving was given over completely to books on occult subjects, books of strange beliefs and even stranger facts, inexplicable to science, books on little-known religious cults; and these were supplemented by huge scrapbooks of clippings from newspapers and magazines, reading which filled me at one and the same time with a sense of premonitory dread and a flame of compulsive joy. For in these prosaically reported facts there lay oddly convincing evidence to augment belief in the myth-pattern to which my uncle had patently subscribed.

After all, the pattern in itself was not new. All religious beliefs, all myth-patterns, in no matter what systems of culture, are basically familiar—they are predicated upon a struggle between forces of good and forces of evil. This pattern was part, too, of my uncle's mythos—the Great Old Ones and the Elder Gods, who may, for all I could figure out, have been the same, represented primal good; the Ancient Ones, primal evil. As in many cultures, the Elder Gods were not often named; the Ancient Ones were, and often, for they were still worshipped and served by followers throughout earth and among the planetary spaces; and they were aligned not only against the Elder Gods, but also against one another in a ceaseless struggle for ultimate dominion. They were, in brief, representations of elemental forces, and each had his element—Cthulhu of water, Cthugha of fire, Ithaqua of air, Hastur of interplanetary spaces; and others among them belonged to great primal forces—Shub-Niggurath, the Messenger of the Gods, of fertility; Yog-Sothoth, of the time-space continua, Azathoth—in a sense the fountain-head of evil.

Was this pattern after all not familiar? The Elder Gods could so easily have become the Christian Trinity; the Ancient Ones could for most believers have been altered into Sathanus and Beelzebub, Mephistofeles and Azarael. Except that they were co-existent, which disturbed me, though I knew that systems of belief constantly overlapped in the history of mankind.

More—there was certain evidence to show that the Cthulhu myth-pattern had existed not only long before the Christian mythos, but also before that of ancient China and the dawn of mankind, surviving unchanged in remote areas of the earth— among the Tcho-Tcho people of Tibet, and the Abominable Snowmen of the high plateaus of Asia, and a strange sea-dwelling people known as the Deep Ones, who were amphibian hybrids, bred of ancient matings between humanoids and batrachia, mutant developments of the race of man—; surviving with recognizable facets in newer religious symbols—in Quetzalcoatl and others among the Gods of Aztec, Mayan, and Inca religions; in the idols of Easter Island; in the ceremonial masks of the Polynesians and the Northwest Coast Indians, where the tentacle and octopoid shape which were the marks of Cthulhu persisted;—so that in a sense it might be said that the Cthulhu mythos was primal.

Even putting all this into the realm of theory and speculation, I was left with the tremendous amounts of clippings which my uncle had collected. These prosaic newspaper accounts served perhaps more effectively in giving pause to any doubt I might have had because all were so palpably reportorial, for none of my uncle's clippings derived from any sensational source, all came straight from news columns or magazines offering factual material only, like the *National Geographic*. So that I was left asking myself certain searching questions.

What did happen to Johansen and the ship *Emma* if not what he himself set forth? Was any other explanation possible?

And why did the U. S. Government send destroyers and submarines to depth-bomb the ocean about Devil Reef outside the harbor of Innsmouth? And arrest scores of Innsmouth people who were never afterward seen again? And fire the coastal area, destroying scores of others? Why—if it were not true that strange rites were being observed by Innsmouth people who bore a hellish relationship to certain sea-dwellers seen by night at Devil Reef?

And what happened to Wilmarth in the mountain country of Vermont, when he came too close to the truth in his research into the cults of the Ancient Ones? And to certain writers of what purported to be fiction—Lovecraft, Howard, Barlow—and what purported to be science—like Fort—when they came too close to truth? Dead, all of them. Dead or missing, like Wilmarth. Dead before their time, most of them, while still comparatively young men. My uncle had their books—though only Lovecraft and Fort had been extensively published in book form —and they were opened by me and read, with greater perturbation than ever, for the fictions of H. P. Lovecraft had, it seemed to me, the same relation to truth as the facts, so inexplicable to science, reported by Charles Fort. If fiction, Lovecraft's tales were damnably bound to fact—even dismissing Fort's facts, the fact inherent in the myths of mankind; they were quasi-myths themselves, as was the untimely fate of their author, whose early death had already given rise to a score of legends, from among which prosaic fact was ever more and more difficult to discover.

But there was time for me to delve into the secrets of my uncle's books, to read further into his notes. So much was clear —he had belief enough to have begun a search for sunken R'lyeh, the city or the kingdom—one could not be sure which it was, or whether indeed it ringed half the earth from the coast of Massachusetts in the Atlantic to the Polynesian Islands on the Pacific—to which Cthulhu had been banished, dead and yet not dead,—"Dead Cthulhu lies dreaming!"—as it read in more than one account, waiting, biding his time to rise and rebel again, to strike once more for dominion against the rule of the Elder Gods, for a world and universes of his own persuasion— for is it not true that if evil triumphs, then evil becomes the law of life, and it is good that must be fought, the rule of the majority establishing the norm, and other than that being abnormal, or, by the way of mankind, the bad, the abhorrent?

My uncle had sought R'lyeh, and he had written disturbingly of how he had done so. He had gone down into the Atlantic's depths, from his home here on the coast, gone down off Devil's Reef and beyond. But there was no mention of how he had done so. By diving equipment? Bathysphere? Of these I had found no evidence whatsoever at the house. It was on these explorations that he had gone during those periods when he had been so long missing from the house on the coast. And yet there had been no mention of any kind of craft, either, nor had my uncle left any such thing in his estate.

If R'lyeh was the object of my uncle's search, what then was Ada Marsh's? This remained to be seen, and to the end of discovering it, I allowed some of my uncle's least informative notes to lie on the library table on the following day. I managed to watch her when she came upon them, and I was left in no doubt, by her reaction, that this was the object of her search—the cache I had found. She had known of these papers. But how?

I confronted her. Even before I had a chance to speak, she spoke.

"You found them!" she cried.

"How did you know about them?"

"I knew what he was doing."

"The search?"

She nodded.

"You can't believe," I protested.

"How can you be so stupid?" she cried angrily. "Did your parents tell you nothing? Your grandfather? How could you have been raised in darkness?" She came close to me, thrust the papers in her hand at me, and demanded, "Let me see the rest of them."

I shook my head.

"Please! They are of no use to you."

"We shall see."

"Tell me, then—he had begun the search?"

"Yes. But I do not know how. There is neither a diver's suit nor a boat."

At this she favored me with a glance which was a challenging mingling of pity and contempt.

"You have not even read all he had written! You haven't read the books—nothing. Do you know what you're standing on?"

"This rug?" I asked wonderingly.

"No, no—the design, the pattern. It's everywhere. Don't you know why? Because it is the great seal of R'lyeh! So much at least he discovered years ago, and was proud to emblazon it here. You stand on what you seek! Look further and find his ring."

III

After Ada Marsh left that day, I turned once more to my uncle's papers. I did not leave them until long past midnight, but by that time I had gone through most of them cursorily, and

some of them with the closest attention. I found it difficult to
believe what I read, yet clearly my Uncle Sylvan had not only
believed it, but seemed actually to have taken some part in it
himself. He had dedicated himself early in life to the search for
the sunken kingdom, he professed openly a devotion to Cthulhu,
and, most suggestive of all, his writings contained many times
chilling hints of encounters—sometimes in the ocean's depths,
sometimes in the streets of legend-haunted Arkham, an ancient,
gambrel-roofed town which lay inland from Innsmouth, not
far from the coast along the Miskatonic River, or in nearby
Dunwich, or even Innsmouth—with men—or beings which
were not men—I could hardly tell which—who believed as he
did and were bound in the same dark bondage to this resurgent
myth from the distant past.

And yet, despite my iconoclasm, there was, too, an edge of
belief I could not diminish. Perhaps it was because of the
strange insinuations in his notes—the half-statements, which
were meant only for reference to his own knowledge, and thus
never clear, for he referred to something he knew too well to
set down—the insinuations about the unhallowed marriages of
Obadiah Marsh and "three others"—could there have been a
Phillips among them?—and the subsequent discovery of photo-
graphs of the Marsh women, Obadiah's widow—a curiously
flat-faced woman, very dark of skin, with a wide, thin-lipped
mouth—and the younger Marshes, all of whom resembled their
mother—together with odd references to their curious hopping
gait, so much a characteristic of "those who descended from
those who came back alone from the sinking of the *Cory*," as
Uncle Sylvan put it. What he meant to say was unmistakable—
Obadiah Marsh had married in Ponape a woman who was not

a Polynesian, yet lived there, and belonged to a sea-race which was only semi-human, and his children and his children's children had borne the stigmata of that marriage, which had in turn led to the holocaust visited upon Innsmouth in 1928, and to the destruction of so many members of the old Innsmouth families. Though my uncle wrote in the most casual manner, there was horror behind his words, and the echo of disaster rolled out from behind the sentences and paragraphs of his writing.

For these of whom he wrote were allied to the Deep Ones; like them, they were amphibious creatures. Of how far the accursed taint went, he did not speculate, nor was there ever word to settle his own status in relation to them. Captain Obadiah Marsh—presumably also Cyrus Phillips, and two others of the *Cory's* crew who had remained behind in Ponape —certainly shared none of the curious traits of their wives and children; but whether the taint went beyond their children, none could say. Was it this Ada Marsh had meant when she had said to me, "You are one of us!"? Or had she reference to some even darker secret? Presumably my grandfather's abhorrence of the sea was due to his knowledge of his father's deeds; he, at least, had successfully resisted the dark heritage.

But my uncle's papers were on the one hand too diffuse to make a coherent account, and on the other too plain to enlist immediate belief. What disturbed me immediately most of all were the repeated hints that his home, this house, was a "haven," a "point" of contact, an "opening to that which lies below"; and the speculations about the "breathing" of the house and the rocky bluff which were so often to be found in the early pages of his notes, and to which no reference whatsoever was made later on. What he had set down was baffling and challenging, fearsome and wonderful; it filled me with awe and at one and the same time an angry disbelief and a wild wish to believe, to know.

I sought everywhere to find out, but was only baffled the more. People in Innsmouth were close-mouthed; some of them actually shunned me—crossed the street at my approach, and in the Italian district frankly crossed themselves as if to ward off the evil eye. No one offered any information, and even at the public library I could obtain no books or records which might help, for these, the librarian told me, had been confiscated and destroyed by government men after the fire and explosions of 1928. I sought in other places—I learned even darker secrets at Arkham and Dunwich, and in the great library of Miskatonic University found at last the fountainhead of all books of dark lore: the half-fabled *Necronomicon* of the mad Arab, Abdul Alhazred, which I was allowed to read only under the watchful eye of a librarian's assistant.

It was then, two weeks after my discovery of my uncle's papers, that I found his ring. This was where one would least have expected to find it, and yet where it was bound to be—in a small packet of his personal belongings returned to the house by the undertaker and left unwrapped in his bureau drawer. The ring was of silver, a massive thing, inlaid with a milky stone which resembled pearl, but was not, and inlaid with the seal of R'lyeh.

I examined it closely. There was nothing extraordinary about it, save its size—to look upon; the wearing of it, however, carried with it unimaginable results. For I had no sooner put it on my finger than it was as if new dimensions opened up to me—or as if the old horizons were pushed back limitlessly. All my senses were made more acute. The very first thing I noticed was my awareness of the susurrus of the house and the rock, now one with the sea's slow movement; so that it was as if the house and the rock were rising and falling with the movement of the water, and it seemed as if I heard from below the house itself the rushing and retreating of water.

At the same time, and perhaps even more importantly, I was aware of a psychic awakening. With the assumption of the ring, I became cognizant of the pressure of unseen forces, potent beyond the telling, as were this house the focal point of influences beyond my comprehension; I stood, in short, as were I a magnet to draw elemental forces from all about me, and these rushed in upon me with such impress that I felt like an island in the midst of the sea, with a raging hurricane centered upon it, a tempestuous tearing at me until I heard almost with relief the very real sound of a horrible, animal-like voice rising in a ghastly ululation—not from above or beside me, but from below!

I tore the ring from my finger, and at once all subsided. The house and the rock returned to quiet and solitude; the winds and the waters which had moved all about me faded and died away; the voice I had heard retreated and was still; the extra-sensory perception I had experienced was ended, and once more all seemed to lie waiting upon my further act. So my dead uncle's ring was a talisman and a rang of wizardry; it was the key to his knowledge and the door to other realms of being.

It was by means of the ring that I discovered my Uncle's way to the sea. I had long sought the path by which he went to the beach, but there was none sufficiently worn to suggest its constant use. There were paths down the rocky declivity; in some

places steps had been cut long ago, so that a man could reach
the water from the house on the promontory, but there was nowhere a place that might have been used for landing craft. The
shore here was deep; I swam in the waters there several times,
always with a wild sense of exultation, so great was my pleasure
in the sea; but there were many rocks, and such beach as there
was lay away from the promontory, around the coves, either to
north or south, almost too great a distance to swim, unless one
were a very capable swimmer, such as I learned—somewhat to
my surprise—that I was.

I had meant to ask Ada Marsh about the ring. It was she who
had told me of its existence, but ever since that day I had refused her access to my Uncle's papers, she had stopped coming
to the house. True, I had seen her lurking about from time to
time, or spied her car parked along the road which led past my
property rather far to the west of the house, and so knew that
she prowled the vicinity. Once I had gone into Innsmouth to
look for her, but she was not at her home, and my inquiries
brought me only open hostility from most of the populace, and
sly, meaningful glances I could not correctly interpret from
others—those shambling, half-derelict people who lived along
the coast streets and byways.

So it was not due to her help that I found my uncle's way to
the sea. I had put on the ring one day, and, drawn to the sea,
was bent on climbing down to the water's edge, when I found
myself, while in the act of crossing the great central room of the
house, virtually unable to leave it, so strong was its pull upon
the ring. I ceased to try, presently, recognizing that a psychic
force was manifest, and simply stood, waiting for guidance; so
that, when I was impelled toward a singularly repellent work

of carved wood, a primitive piece representing some hideous batrachian hybrid, affixed to a pedestal along one wall of the study, I yielded to impulse, went over to it, seized hold of it, and pushed, pulled, and finally turned it right and left. It gave to the left.

Instantly there was a creaking of chains, a clanking of gears, and the entire section of the study floor covered by the rug bearing the seal of R'lyeh came up like a great trap-door. I went wonderingly over to it, my pulse quickening with excitement. And I looked down into the pit below—a great, yawning depth, into the darkness of which a continuing spiral of steps had been hewn out of the solid rock upon which the house stood. Did it lead to water below? I selected a book at random from my uncle's set of Dumas and dropped it; then I stood listening for any sound from below. It came at last: a splash—distantly.

So, with the utmost caution, I crept down the interminable stairs, down into the smell of the sea—small wonder I had felt that the sea was in the house!—down into the dank coolness of a watery place, until I could feel the moisture on the walls and the steps underfoot, down into the sound of restless water below, the sloshing and rushing of the sea, until I came to where the stairs ended, at the very edge of the water, in a kind of cavern that was large enough to have held the entire house in which my Uncle Sylvan had lived. And I knew beyond cavil that this was my uncle's way to the sea, this and no other; though I was as mystified as ever to find even here no evidence of boat or diving gear, but only footprints—and, seen in the light of the matches I struck, something more—the long, slithered marks and the blobs where some monstrous entity had rested, marks which made me to think with prickling scalp and goose-fleshed skin of some of those hideous representations brought to the great room above me by my Uncle Sylvan and others before him from the mysterious islands of Polynesia.

How long I stood there, I do not know. For there, at the water's edge, with the ring bearing the seal of R'lyeh on my finger, I heard from the depths of the water below sounds of movement and life, coming from a great distance indeed, from outward, which is to say, from the direction of the sea, and from below, so that I suspected the existence of some sort of passage to the sea, either immediately at hand, by means of a subaqueous cavern, or below this level, for the cavern in which I stood was ringed around, so far as I could see in the wan glow of the matches I lit, with solid rock, and the movement of the water indicated the movement of the sea, which could not have been coincidental. So the opening was outward, and I must find it without delay.

I climbed back up the stairs, closed the opening once more, and hurried to my car for a journey to Boston. I returned late that night with a diving helmet and a portable oxygen tank, ready to descend next day into the sea below the house. I removed the ring no more, and that night I dreamed great dreams of ancient lore, of cities on distant stars and magnificent spired settlements in far, fabulous places of the earth—in the unknown Antarctic, high in mountainous Tibet, far beneath the surface of the sea; I dreamed that I moved among great dwellings in wonder and beauty, amidst others of my kind, and among aliens as friends, aliens whose very aspect might, in waking hours, have congealed the blood in my veins, all here in this nocturnal world given to one cause, the service to those great ones whose minions we were; dreamed through the night of other worlds, other realms of being; of new sensations and incredible, tentacled beings commanding our obedience and worship; dreamed so that I woke next morning exhausted and yet exhilarated, as if in the night I had actually experienced my dreams and yet remained charged with unimaginable strength for greater ordeals to come.

But I was on the threshold of a greater discovery.

Late the next afternoon, I donned my swimming trunks, affixed a pair of flippers to my feet, put on the helmet and oxygen tanks, and descended to the water's edge below the house. Even now I find it difficult to write of what befell me without wonder and incredulity. I lowered myself cautiously into that water, feeling for bottom, and, finding it, walked outward toward the sea, at the bottom of a cavern many times the height of a man, walked outward until suddenly I came to its end, and there, without warning, I stepped off into space, and fell slowly through the water toward the ocean floor, a grey world of rocks and sand and aquatic growth that wove and writhed eerily in the dim light which penetrated that depth.

Here I was sharply conscious of the water's pressure, and beginning to wonder, too, about the weight of the helmet and oxygen tank when the time came for me to rise again. Perhaps the need of finding some place by means of which to walk out on to the shore would preclude any further search; yet, even as I thought this, I was impelled ever outward, walking away from the shore and bearing south, out from Innsmouth.

It dawned upon me with horrifying suddenness that I was being drawn as by a magnet, even against my better judgment, for the oxygen in my tanks would not last long, and would need to be replenished before I could hope to return, if I went very far out from the shore line. Yet I was helpless to prevent myself from going seaward; it was as if some power beyond my control were drawing me away from the shore, outward and down, for the land beneath the sea there sloped gently downward, in a direction southeast of the house on the rock; in this direction I went steadily now, without pause, even though I was aware of a growing panic—I must turn about, must begin to find my way back. To swim up to the cave would require almost superhuman effort, despite the lightening pressure of the depths to start me on my way; to reach the foot of the stairs in the pit below the house, at a time when my oxygen was surely all but gone, would be almost impossible, if I did not turn without delay.

Yet something there was would not permit me to turn. I moved ever onward, outward, as if by a design imposed upon me by a power greater than my own. I had no alternative, I must go ahead, and all the while my alarm grew, I found myself in violent conflict between what I wished to do and what I must do, and the oxygen in my tanks diminished with every step. Several times I vaulted upward, swimming vigorously; but, while there was no difficulty about swimming—indeed, I seemed to swim with almost miraculous ease—always I came back to the ocean floor, or found myself swimming outward.

Once I paused and looked about me, trying in vain to pierce the ocean's depths. I thought I imagined a great pale green fish swimming in my wake, and had the illusion that it was a mermaid, for I seemed to see hair streaming from it; but then it was lost again behind the growths of that aquatic deep. But I could not pause for long; I was drawn ever forward, until at last I knew that my oxygen was almost gone, my breathing became more and more labored, and I struggled to swim to the surface, only to find myself falling from the place to which I had vaulted upward, falling into a crevice on the ocean's floor.

Then, only a few moments before I lost consciousness, I was aware of the swift approach of my follower, of hands upon my helmet and the oxygen tanks—it was not a fish at all, nor a mermaid: it was the naked body of Ada Marsh I had seen, with her long hair streaming out behind her, swimming with the ease and facility of a natural denizen of the deep!

IV

What followed upon this almost dreamlike vision was most incredible of all. I felt in my declining consciousness, rather than saw, that Ada took the helmet and oxygen tanks from me and dropped them into the depths below, and then, slowly, awareness returned; I found myself swimming, with Ada guiding me with her strong, capable fingers, not back, not up, but still outward. And I found myself swimming as ably as she, and, like herself, opening and closing my mouth as were I breathing through the water—*and so I was!* What ancestral gift I had unwittingly possessed now opened up before me all the vast wonders of the sea—I could breathe without surfacing, an amphibian born!

Ada flashed ahead of me, and I followed. I was swift, but she was swifter. No more the slow walk across the ocean's floor, now only the propulsion of arms and legs that were seemingly made for the water, and the surging, triumphant joy of swimming so, without constraint, toward some goal I knew dimly I was meant to reach. Ada led the way, and I followed,

while above us, beyond the water, the sun sank westward, and
the day ended, the last light withdrew down the west, and the
sickle moon shone in the afterglow.

And at this hour we drove upward toward the surface, following a line of jagged rock which marked the wall of shore
or island, I could not tell which, and broke water far from the
shore at a place where a shelf of land jutted out of the sea,
from which it was possible to see to the west the twinkling
lights of a town, a harbor city, seeing which, and looking back
to where Ada Marsh and I sat in the moonlight, with boats
moving shadowily between us and the shore, and between us
and the line of the horizon to the east, I knew where we were
—on that same Devil Reef off Innsmouth, the place where once
before, prior to that catastrophic night in 1928, our ancestors
had played and disported themselves among their brethren
from the ocean's deeps.

"How could you have failed to know?" asked Ada patiently.
"You might have died with all that to suffocate you. If I had
not come to the house when I did. . . ."

"I had no way of knowing," I said.

"How else did you think your uncle went exploring, but like
this?"

My Uncle Sylvan's quest was hers, too, and now it was mine.
To look for the seal of R'lyeh, and beyond, to discover the
sleeper in the depths, the dreamer whose call I had felt and
answered—great Cthulhu. It was not off Innsmouth, of that
Ada was confident. And to prove it, she led the way down into
the depths once more, far down off Devil Reef and showed
me the great megalithic stone structures lying in ruin there as
a result of the depth-bombing of 1928, the place where many

years before the early Marshes and Phillipses had continued
their contact with the Deep Ones, down to swim among the
ruins of that once great city, where I saw the first of them
and was filled with horror at the sight—the frog-like caricature
of a human being, that swam with greatly exaggerated move-
ments so similar to those of a frog, and watched us with
bulging eyes and batrachian mouth, boldly, not fearful, recognizing us as his brethren from outside, down through the
monoliths to the ocean floor once more. The destruction there
was very great. Even so had other places been destroyed by
little bands of wilful men dedicated to preventing the return
of great Cthulhu.

And so up again, and back to the house on the rock, where
Ada had left her clothes, and to make that compact which
bound us each to each, and to plan for the journey to Ponape
and the further search.

Within two weeks we were off to Ponape in a chartered
craft, off on that mission of which we dared breathe no word
to the ship's crew, for fear they would think us mad and
desert. We were confident that our quest would be successful,
that somewhere in the uncharted islands of the Polynesias we
would find that which we sought, and, finding it, go to join
forever our brethren of the seas who serve and wait upon
the day of the resurrection, when Cthulhu and Hastur and
Lloigor and Yog-Sothoth shall rise again and vanquish the
Elder Gods in that titanic struggle which must come.

We made Ponape our headquarters. Sometimes we set out
from there; sometimes we used the craft we had chartered,
oblivious of the curiosity of the crew. We searched the waters;
sometimes we were gone for days. And soon my metamorphosis

was complete. I dare not tell how we sustained ourselves in those journeys under the sea, of what manner of food we ate. Once there was a crash of a great air liner . . . but of this, no more. Suffice it to say that we survived, and I found myself doing things I would have thought bestial only a year ago, that nothing but the urgence of our quest impelled us on, and nothing other concerned us—only our survival, and the goal we held ever before our eyes.

How shall I write of what we saw and still retain even a shred of confidence and trust? The great cities of the ocean floor, and the greatest of them all, the most ancient, off the coast from Ponape, where the Deep Ones abounded, and we could move for days among the towers and the great slabs of stone, down among the minarets and domes of that sunken city, almost lost among the aquatic forest-growth of the bottom of the sea, seeing how the Deep Ones lived, befriending and befriended by a curious marine life which was octopoid in general appearance, and yet was not octopoid, fighting sharks and other enemies, even as we were forced to do from time to time, living only to serve him whose call can be heard in the depths, though none knows where he lies dreaming against the time of his coming again.

How shall I write of our ceaseless search, from city to city, from building to building, looking always for the great seal, beneath which He may lie, save as an endless round of days and nights, sustained by hope and the driving urgence of the goal which loomed always ahead, a little closer every day? It seldom varied, and yet was always different. None could tell what each new day would bring. True, our chartered craft was not always a boon, for we were required to leave it by boat, and in turn, once our boat could be concealed along some island shore, to go into the depths surreptitiously, which displeased us. Even so, the crew grew daily more inquisitive, confident that we sought hidden treasure, and likely to demand a share, so that it was difficult avoiding their questions and their ever increasing suspicions.

We sought thus for three months, and then, two days ago, we put down anchor off a strange, uninhabited island far from any major settlement. Nothing grew upon it, and it had the appearance of blasted area. Indeed, it seemed to be but an upthrusting of basaltic rock, which at one time must have loomed high above the water, but which had been bombarded severely, possibly during the past war. Here we left our craft, went round the island, and descended into the sea. There, too, was a city of the Deep Ones, and it, too, had been blasted and ruined by enemy action.

But, though the city below the black island was in ruins, it was not deserted, and it stretched away on all sides into untouched areas. And there, in one of the oldest of the huge, monolithic buildings, we found that which we sought—in the center of a vast room, many storeys in height, lay a great stone slab which was the source of that likeness I had first seen and failed to recognize in the decorations of my uncle's house —the Seal of R'lyeh! And, standing upon it, we could hear from beneath it, movement as of some vast amorphous body, restless as the sea, stirring in dream—and we knew we had come to the goal we sought, and could now enter upon an eternity of service to Him Who Will Rise Again, the dweller in the deep, the sleeper in the depths, whose dreams encompass not only earth but the dominion of all the universes, and who shall need such as Ada Marsh and I to minister to his wants until the time of his second coming.

We are still here as I write, and I set this down should we fail to return to our craft. The hour is late, and tomorrow we shall descend again, to find some way, if possible, to open the seal. Was it indeed imposed upon Great Cthulhu by the Elder Gods in banishing him? And dare we then to pry it up, to go below, into the presence of Him Who Lies Dreaming there? Ada and I—and soon there will be another of us, born in his natural element, to wait and serve Great Cthulhu. For we have heard the call, we have obeyed, and we are not alone. There are others who come from every corner of the earth, spawn too of that mating between men and the women of the sea, and soon the seas will belong to us, and thereafter all earth, and beyond . . . and we shall live in power and glory forever.

*   *   *

Extract from the Singapore *Times,* November 7, 1947.

The crew of the ship *Rogers Clark* were freed today after being held in connection with the strange disappearance of Mr. and Mrs. Marius Phillips, who had chartered the vessel to conduct some kind of research among the Polynesias. Mr. and Mrs. Phillips were last seen in the vicinity of an uninhabited island approximately South Latitude 47° 53', West Longitude 127° 37'. They had gone out in a small boat and evidently entered the island from the shore opposite their ship. From the island they would seem to have gone into the sea, for the crew testified to witnessing a singularly astonishing upheaval of the water on the far side of the island, and the ship's captain, together with the first mate, who were on the bridge, saw what appeared to be both his employers tossed aloft in the geyser of water and drawn back down again into the sea. They did not reappear, though the ship stood by for several hours. An examination of the island disclosed that the clothes worn by Mr. and Mrs. Phillips were in their small boat. A manuscript in Mr. Phillips' hand, purporting to be fact, but obviously fiction, was found in his cabin, and turned in to the Singapore police by Captain Morton. No trace of Mr. and Mrs. Phillips has been found. . . .

SCIENCE FICTION, FANTASY, AND HORROR AVAILABLE FROM CARROLL & GRAF

☐ Simak, Clifford D. / Cemetery World   3.50
☐ Simak, Clifford D. / The Werewolf Principle   3.95
☐ Stableford, Brian / The Angel of Pain   5.95
☐ Stableford, Brian / The Carnival of Destruction   5.95
☐ Stableford, Brian / The Walking Shadow   3.95
☐ Stableford, Brian / The Werewolves of London   4.95
☐ Stoker, Bram / Jewel of Seven Stars   3.95
☐ Sturgeon, Theodore / The Dreaming Jewels   3.95
☐ Sturgeon, Theodore / More Than Human   3.95
☐ Sturgeon, Theodore / Some of Your Blood   3.95
☐ van Vogt, A. E. / Cosmic Encounter   3.95
☐ van Vogt, A. E. / The House That Stood Still   3.95
☐ Watson, Ian / The Embedding   3.95
☐ Wyndham, John / The Chrysalids   3.95
☐ Wyndham, John / The Day of the Triffids   3.95